THE HOLIDAY FIVE

TRICK OR TROUBLE?

BY ILENE COOPER

VIKING

VIKING

Published by the Penguin Group

Penguin Books USA Inc., 375 Hudson Street, New York, New York 10014, U.S.A.

Penguin Books Ltd, 27 Wrights Lane, London W8 5TZ, England

Penguin Books Australia Ltd, Ringwood, Victoria, Australia

Penguin Books Canada Ltd, 10 Alcorn Avenue, Toronto, Ontario, Canada M4V 3B2

Penguin Books (N.Z.) Ltd, 182–190 Wairau Road, Auckland 10, New Zealand

Penguin Books Ltd, Registered Offices: Harmondsworth, Middlesex, England

First published in 1994 by Viking, a division of Penguin Books USA Inc.

1 3 5 7 9 10 8 6 4 2

Library of Congress Cataloging-in-Publication Data

Cooper, Ilene.

Trick or trouble? / Ilene Cooper.   p.   cm. — (The Holiday Five)

Summary: Lia makes four new friends at summer camp, but when they
come to her house in Maple Park, Illinois, at Halloween, she worries that
they will discover that she is not so popular in her seventh grade class.

ISBN 0-670-85208-2

[1. Friendship—Fiction.   2. Schools—Fiction.]

I. Title.   II. Series: Cooper, Ilene. Holiday Five.

PZ7.C7856Tp   1994   [Fic]—dc20   93-41477   CIP   AC

Printed in U.S.A.   Set in 11 pt. Century

ONE

Lia Greene reached into the back of the drawer. "Oh, yuck!" She pulled out a crumpled ball of green material, a little damp, and covered with sand.

"What is it?" Jill Lewis asked, wrinkling her nose.

Maddy Donaldson stopped her packing for a moment. "What *was* it, you mean."

"Remember when I couldn't find the bottom of my two-piece bathing suit?" Lia held the offending material with two fingers. "I think I found it. Now what do I do with it?"

"Rinse it out," Erin Moriarity advised.

"*Throw* it out," Katherine Wallace countered.

It was easy to figure out who came from a wealthy society family and who was here on scholarship, Lia thought. Erin could never afford to be so casual about an item of clothing. But even though Kathy had brought enough bathing suits to outfit a couple of cabins and lived in one of Chicago's ritziest suburbs, she wasn't a snob. If anything, Kathy was careful not to flaunt the fact she had money. Sometimes, though, her casual comments gave her away.

Lia put the suit in a plastic bag. She'd deal with it later. "I'm tired," she complained. "I feel like I've been sorting through stuff for days."

"It's been about an hour," Erin said.

"Why is packing to come to camp so much fun, and packing to go home such a drag?" Maddy asked, swallowing a bite of the cookie that was getting crumbs all over her clothes—both the ones she had on and the ones she was stuffing into a bag.

"That's simple," Jill said, putting a couple of sweat-shirts into her trunk. "Because it's all over, finished, done. Now it's back to school, homework, chores." She pretended to tear out her curly black hair by its roots.

"Come on," Lia said. "You've got your ice-skating waiting, too. You must be looking forward to that."

"Yeah," Jill admitted. "I've missed it. I hope I haven't gotten too rusty."

Lia had been impressed when she learned that Jill had won several prizes for her ice-skating. "You'll get right back to it," Lia said encouragingly.

Jill held up crossed fingers.

Erin glanced at her watch. "We'd better get this stuff packed. It's almost time for dinner. We don't want to be late."

"Our last night. Maybe they'll have something decent for a change," Kathy said as she threw some pajamas in the direction of her trunk.

"They've had all summer to get it right," Jill said dryly.

Maddy shrugged. "Oh, the food hasn't been that bad."

Lia and Jill exchanged glances behind Maddy's back. That said it all. Maddy had never met a meal she didn't like. Even the camp's meat loaf that looked more like a sponge than something edible disappeared off Maddy's plate. Lia was going home even skinnier than when she arrived, because the one bad thing about Camp Wildwood was the food. Lia was never sure how Maddy was able to wolf it down.

If Lia and Jill were too polite to say anything, Erin wasn't. "Yeah, the meals haven't been that bad if you don't mind eating dog food."

"Erin!" Lia hoped Erin hadn't hurt Maddy's feelings. But Erin just shrugged and said, "It's true."

To the casual observer, Erin looked like a little pixie, but Erin was tough. Maybe it was because she was one of six children and had to stand up for herself if she wanted to be heard at all. Or maybe growing up in the city just made you more able to deal with stuff. Either way, Erin always spoke her mind.

"Hey, do I have a hole in my T-shirt or something?" Erin asked Lia. "You're staring at me."

Lia sat down on the bed. "I guess I was thinking about the first time I saw you, at the bus station. You looked like you were on your way to a firing squad, not camp."

"Well, excuse me. I had never been to camp before. If it hadn't been for that grant from Family Services, I wouldn't be here now. Then I walk into Bunk Three, and I'm in the middle of a big reunion."

"We had never bunked together before," Maddy pointed out.

"No, but you knew each other last year. And you all looked pretty chummy to me when I wandered in. There I was, a poor kid from the city, friendless, alone," she said dramatically.

"Oh, you're breaking my heart," Kathy laughed.

"Didn't even know enough to pack a trunk. I brought my stuff in a cardboard box," she continued.

Lia had to give Erin credit. She never seemed very embarrassed about having less money than the rest of them. If anything, she played on her tough city-kid image, teasing the others about their soft lives.

"Well, you didn't let your humble status hold you down," Jill pointed out. "You're a sure bet to win the swimming trophy."

Erin looked at her clothes strewn around the floor. "Too bad I didn't win a trunk. Here I am packing cardboard boxes again."

"You'll know better next summer," Kathy told her.

"I'm not sure that trunks are in the Moriarity family budget."

"So I'll lend you one." Kathy shrugged.

"Hey, it looks like a tornado went through this room." Bunk Three's counselor, Ellen Reiter, stood in the doorway surveying the room with dismay. "You guys are supposed to be packed before dinner. And it's my neck if you aren't."

"You could have stayed and helped us," Erin said.

"Ellen had more important things to do," Maddy giggled. "She had to say good-bye to Tommy Finelli."

Ellen pretended to swat her with the sweater she

was carrying. "You're a big girl, you do your own packing."

Bunk Three had lucked out when they got Ellen for a counselor. She was nice, most of the time, and fun. From the first week, it had been clear that Tommy, one of the boys' counselors, liked Ellen, and by the second week, she liked him too. Bunk Three had followed the romance with interest. Once they had even snuck out after curfew and followed Ellen and Tommy down to the lake. Unfortunately, Maddy had tripped over a log, alerting the counselors to their presence. That had been the only time they had seen Ellen mad all summer, and boy had she been hot.

"So are you going to see Tommy when camp is over?" Lia asked with interest.

"Probably as often as you five will see each other."

"We'll see each other," Lia protested.

"That's what everybody thinks," Ellen said a little sadly. "But you go home, and you get caught up in your regular lives. It'll be next summer before you all get together again. Now, hurry up. The banquet starts in fifteen minutes."

As soon as Ellen closed the door, Maddy said, "I

don't think that was a very nice thing to say. How does she know we won't get together?"

"I think she was more worried about her and Tommy than she was about us," Kathy noted.

"But she's probably right," Erin said. "Did you guys see each other last year?"

Lia and Kathy looked at each other. "Well, we talked about it," Lia said, "but we never got around to it. We talked on the phone a couple of times."

Erin shrugged. "See what I mean?"

"If we want to visit each other, we just need to do a little planning," Lia said.

"A little? Maybe if we lived near each other . . ." Maddy's voice trailed off.

"We're not so far apart," Kathy replied. "Erin lives in Chicago, Maddy's in Waukegan, and the rest of us live in the suburbs."

Jill asked if anyone had seen her green socks, changing the subject, but Lia decided she wasn't about to let her cabinmates drift off for the winter without making some concrete plans. She was determined to come up with an idea that would get them all together on a regular basis.

The girls put on the fresh T-shirts that the camp had

given out to be worn to the evening's banquet. Lia asked Kathy to French braid her hair, and Erin found some gel in her drawer and gave her short, copper-colored hair a spiked do.

"What do you think?" Erin asked, twirling around so everyone could get a good look.

"You look like you got your finger caught in an electric socket," Maddy finally said.

Erin's mouth formed a little *O*, then she started laughing. "Guess you're getting me back for the dog food remark. Well, that's okay. I think my hair looks good anyway."

As the girls headed outside, Lia thought to herself that one of the things she liked best about her cabin-mates was that they never really got mad at each other. They might get even, but they didn't get mad.

"I hope I get to say good-bye to Beauty tomorrow," Maddy said, looking over toward the barn.

"Do you really think a horse is going to miss you?" Erin asked.

"I'm going to miss her."

Together they filed into the dining room. The large room, with its picnic-style tables, was full of kids getting settled at the places they had occupied all summer. Except for meals and the campfires, the boys and girls didn't see that much of each other. Still, some alliances had been formed. Marty Robertson had developed a real thing for Kathy. He had even managed to sneak a box of candy into the cabin. Lia saw him now, searching the room to find her.

"He's looking for you," Lia said, poking Kathy.

"Who?" Kathy said, innocently.

"Luke Perry," Erin laughed.

Kathy gave her a withering look and took her usual rickety seat at table three.

Mrs. Tillman, the short, stocky owner of the camp, strode to the front of the room, where a microphone had been set up. "Good evening, campers. Well, here we are at the end of another summer. I hope you have had a good time."

There were claps and whistles from the assembled crowd.

"We've planned a special dinner for you all."

"I'll be the judge of that," Erin whispered to Lia.

"And then," Mrs. Tillman continued, "we'll hand out the camp awards. So enjoy."

By the time dinner was finished, even Erin had to admit her tummy was satisfied. The camp cook must have left a day early, because dinner consisted of fried chicken from a local take-out place, mashed potatoes, and ice cream sundaes for dessert.

"Why couldn't they have done this earlier in the summer?" Jill asked.

"Because then we'd have wanted to go home even less than we do now," Lia informed her.

"Mrs. Tillman just wanted to leave us with good memories of the food," Kathy said. "That way, when we get home tomorrow and our parents ask us how the meals were, we'll say great."

"My memory's not that short," Erin muttered.

Mrs. Tillman came back to the microphone. "Before we hand out the awards, I have a special treat for you all. The counselors have gotten together and written a good-bye song."

The twelve counselors, six male, six female, formed a line and, at Tommy Finelli's cue, began snapping their fingers and rapping.

> *Camp is over;*
> *We had some fun.*
> *Four long weeks*
> *In the summer sun.*
> *So that you can keep it straight,*
> *Now we're gonna recapitulate.*

They went on to add a number of verses recalling all the funny things that had happened at camp. Like the day that a group of girls snuck into the cook's room so they could catch up on *All My Children*, and a counselor called the police because she thought they were missing.

The kids thought the whole thing was a hoot. Mrs. Tillman, a frown creasing her face, looked like she didn't think it was quite so funny, but she tried to be a good sport. She led the applause when the counselors were finished.

"Well, I had no idea we had such a talented group of counselors. I also had no idea that some of these incidents occurred. But that's camp, I guess. Now, it's time for the last official function of camp, the annual awards."

There was a long list of them. Erin did win the swimming trophy, and Kathy won one for horseback riding. There were awards for the most talented camper, the most athletic camper, even the messiest camper, a boy from Cabin Ten who was rumored to have worn the same socks all summer.

Lia was daydreaming when she heard her name called. "What did Mrs. Tillman say?" she asked, just as Jill gave her a poke in the side.

"You won!" Maddy said excitedly.

"Won what?"

"All-around camper," Kathy told her. "Go get your trophy."

Lia walked up to the front of the room in a daze.

"Lia, not only have you been one of our most popular campers, you were an active participant in our plays and athletic teams, and you even ran the camp library for us. You're universally well liked among your fellow campmates. I think the counselors who chose you made an excellent choice." She handed Lia the biggest trophy that had been given all evening.

Flushed with excitement and embarrassment, Lia stood and watched as the kids gave her a rousing round of applause. Ducking her head a little, she took her trophy and practically ran back to her chair, where her bunkmates were waiting with smiles and hugs.

"All right!" Jill whispered.

"Let me see it," Erin demanded.

Lia handed over the trophy as Mrs. Tillman called for the assembled audience to stand and sing the camp song, "O Wildwood." Lia sang automatically, all the while trying to get her mind around the fact that she had been named all-around camper. She had never expected this, never even thought about it. She had loved being in the camp shows and had participated eagerly in all the activities. And "universally popular with the other kids," Mrs. Tillman had said! Lia knew she had made a lot of friends, but that was because most of the kids were so nice. She'd never dreamed that her summer would end up like this.

Finally, it was over. Lia and the girls wandered back to the bunk. When they were inside, and sitting comfortably on their beds, Kathy said, "Pass it around, Lia."

Lia dutifully handed the trophy to Jill.

"Oh, the honor you've brought to our bunk," Jill told her with mock seriousness.

"Queen of Camp Wildwood," Kathy agreed.

"How is she going to top this next year?" Erin wondered. "Maybe she can replace Mrs. Tillman."

Lia didn't mind the good-natured teasing. "Oh, you guys are just jealous. You wish you were taking home this big trophy."

"I don't have room for it in my cardboard box," Erin informed her.

"Hey, we've got something more important than this trophy to talk about," Lia said.

"What's that?" Maddy asked.

"How are we going to make sure we see each other

during the year," Lia replied. "I don't want Ellen's prediction to come true."

Maddy flopped down on her bed. "We'll call and set something up."

"Not good enough." Lia took her trophy and put it on her dresser. "Let's make a plan."

"Shall we just set a date?" Kathy asked.

"But when?" Jill wondered. "We've all got different schedules and different days off from school."

Lia had a brainstorm. "I know. Let's get together on holidays."

"Holidays?" Kathy asked with a frown. "We have to spend holidays with our families."

"I don't mean big holidays like Thanksgiving. But what about Halloween?"

Jill went over to the wall and pulled down the calendar. She flipped the pages to October. "It's on a Saturday this year."

"That's a great idea," Maddy said enthusiastically. "It would be fun to spend Halloween together. Now, whose house should we go to?"

Lia spoke up. "Maple Park goes all out for Halloween. There are hayrides in the park, and costume contests, and everybody goes to the community center for a party at night."

The girls agreed this sounded like fun.

"Say, why don't you guys come up on Friday?" Lia said, warming to her idea. "That way we can have the whole weekend together."

"Is this going to be a one-time-only thing?" Erin asked. "Or are we going to try and do it all year?"

"I'm sure we can manage a couple of times during the year," Kathy said.

"And we won't forget if it's always around holidays," Maddy added.

"It's kind of like a club," Erin said. "I've never been in a club before."

Lia looked around with satisfaction. "Just call us the Holiday Five."

Two

Lia looked out the window of the camp bus. Rain streaked the glass, blurring the fields and houses as the bus rolled by. She was glad the day was so cold and crummy. It suited her mood.

Maybe it was normal to feel let down after such a big evening. The girls had been so psyched, they'd stayed up most of the night talking, giggling, and reminiscing. Ellen, who had gotten in awfully late, had weakly told them a couple of times to keep it down, before falling asleep herself.

All of them, even Ellen, had woken up late and groggy. The trunks had been taken to the buses during last night's dinner, so the girls only had a few items to keep track of as they were rushing around to leave. Even those proved too many.

"Where's my toothbrush?" Maddy yelled from the bathroom. "It's missing."

"I don't think anyone stole it," Kathy said grumpily.

"Maybe you packed it," Jill suggested.

Maddy stuck her head out the door, a glum expression on her face. "I did pack it. I stuck it in a plastic bag with my hairbrush. My hairbrush!" Maddy groaned. "I don't have that either."

"Well, I'll lend you a hairbrush," Lia said. "A toothbrush—I don't think so."

"What am I supposed to do? I can't get on the bus with dragon breath."

"If you do, sit next to Rebecca Royce," Erin said, looking up from tying her shoe. "That girl's been bugging me all summer."

"Just rub some toothpaste on your finger," Lia suggested.

"That's a good idea but I . . . I think I packed my toothpaste, too," Maddy admitted.

Jill tossed a tube at her. Then they had all gotten silly. Erin threw a pair of dirty socks she had found under her bed, and suddenly the girls were throwing all kinds of leftovers at each other—torn T-shirts, single house slippers, even empty bags of potato chips.

Lia sighed and turned away from the bus window. It was raining harder now, and she couldn't see anything.

Kathy was sitting next to her. "What's wrong?" she asked, her eyes closed.

"I thought you were sleeping."

Kathy sat up. "Not really. So what's the problem?"

"I don't know. Everything seems blah."

"Well, it's too bad camp's over. But it will be fun to get home. I can't wait to see my friends."

"Mmm," Lia responded.

It was so ironic. Lia glanced down at the shopping bag that held her all-around camper trophy and the other things she had packed up this morning. At camp she had been one of the most popular kids, and she had the trophy to prove it. Wouldn't everybody be surprised to find out that at home she was a big nobody.

It hadn't always been that way. Before last year, Lia had been friendly with most of the girls. There hadn't been any cliques. Then, right before Christmas, Eden Aspinall had arrived. She had taken the sixth grade by storm with just the right clothes and just the right amount of indifference. Within weeks, most of the girls were elbowing each other aside to be her partner in science class or sit next to her on the bus.

Lia didn't get it. Privately, she called Eden Bossy the Cow, but with a dizzying suddenness, Eden's interests became everyone's and Eden's biggest interest was boys. At first, Lia had tried to muster up some enthusiasm, just to be part of the crowd, but soon it just became too hard to try. As the school year progressed, Lia saw less and less of her friends.

She had spent most of her time doing her homework, which was good for her grades, but awfully lonely. Ironically, about the only person she saw on a regular basis was a boy, her next-door neighbor, Scott Tierney. They had a lot in common. They both collected stamps and liked the same television shows and were crazy about their dogs. It wasn't the same as having girlfriends, though.

Lia didn't like the situation, but her mother hated it. Lia couldn't hide the fact that the girls weren't calling her, and Mrs. Greene kept asking her what happened. Lia tried to explain about Eden, but her mother seemed to put the blame on Lia.

"Call some of the girls. Invite them over," Mrs. Greene urged.

Sometimes Lia called. Mostly, she just pretended to. Lia knew the girls were too busy to make room for her. Besides, she was embarrassed to seem so needy. If any of the girls were interested in seeing her, they knew her phone number.

Except for the time she spent with Scott, Lia figured that all she had to look forward to was another year of doing her homework, visiting her grandmother, and coming up with ways to tell her parents nicely that she didn't want to go to the movies or the mall or the library with them.

If only she could stay at camp all year, Lia thought with a sigh. She hadn't told anyone at Wildwood about what her life was like at home. For one thing, she'd been having so much fun, home seemed very far away. For another, what exactly was she going to say? I'm glad you all think I'm swell, but if you lived in Maple Park, you probably wouldn't know I'm alive?

As the summer passed, Lia had allowed herself to forget about how things were at home. Now, though, with the bus speeding south, all the lonely feelings of last year began to envelop her. Her mood was as gray as the sky. She considered confiding in Kathy, but when she turned to her, it was clear from Kathy's heavy breathing that she had finally fallen asleep.

Pulling a small notepad and pencil from her bag, Lia began to draw a crude map. At the top was Wisconsin with a little dot to indicate Camp Wildwood. Then she drew a crooked line to stand for Lake Michigan. One thing that was going to make the Holiday Five possible was that all the girls lived along Lake Michigan, and there was a commuter train that went all the way from Waukegan, where Maddy lived, near the Illinois-Wisconsin border, to downtown Chicago, where Erin could get the train.

Lia put a star by Waukegan and wrote in Maddy's name. Then, guessing at the distance, she labeled Lake Pointe, Kathy's elegant suburb. Maple Park was a little farther south, then came Evanston where Jill lived. It was the suburb right next to Chicago. Northwestern University was there, and even though it was considered a suburb, it was bigger than some cities. Lia wasn't quite sure where Erin lived in Chicago. Lia had been there lots of times, of course, but almost always to go shopping downtown or to see the museums or the aquarium. She hadn't spent much time in the neighborhoods.

Tracing her finger down the towns from Waukegan to Chicago, Lia felt a little better. She and her friends really weren't going to be that far apart. Why, she could just jump on a train and see any one of them. Not that her mother would be that keen about her taking the train alone. But it was possible, and just that possibility perked her up.

"Wau-ke-gan!" the bus driver called into his microphone.

Lia gave Kathy a little shake. The bus made only three stops, where they'd be met by their parents: Waukegan, Evanston, and Chicago. Kathy was assigned to get off in Waukegan.

"We're here?" Kathy yawned.

"Yeah. You'd better hurry."

"The bus won't leave until I'm off," Kathy said, but she did move a little faster as she grabbed her jacket and her duffle bag.

Maddy, who had been sitting a few rows back with Jill, was getting off too. On her way down the aisle, she stopped to lean over and give Lia a little hug.

"I'll talk to you soon."

"Real soon," Lia promised.

Kathy followed with a hug of her own. "See you at Halloween."

There was a flurry of kids disembarking. In a few seconds Kathy and Maddy were gone.

Lia looked around and decided to go sit across from Erin and next to Jill in the seat vacated by Maddy. She glanced at her watch. About another forty-five minutes and they'd be in Evanston, where she and Jill would get off. That's where her parents would meet her and take her home.

"Lia, you've barely said anything about camp," her mother said, turning around to look at her daughter in the back seat.

"She's barely said anything," Mr. Greene noted.

Lia didn't really feel like talking, but it didn't seem fair to take her mood out on her parents.

"I won a trophy at the banquet last night."

"You did!" her mother exclaimed. "For what?"

"All-around camper."

"That sounds like a pretty big deal," her father said.

Lia shrugged. "I guess." Somehow, with everything familiar around her, it didn't seem like one. Not the way it had last night, anyway.

"Where is it?" Mrs. Greene asked.

Lia pulled the trophy out of her bag and handed it over to her mother.

"Lia, this is terrific," Mrs. Greene said, very impressed.

"You must have been very popular with the other campers to have won this."

"I got along pretty well with everyone."

"Well, with something like this under your belt, I can't believe that you're going to have the same kind of trouble at school that you did last year."

"It's completely different, Mom."

"I don't see how. If you can make friends at camp, you can make friends at home."

Why didn't parents get it? Lia wondered. Camp wasn't like school. It was as if she could be a different person there. At home she was just the same old Lia Greene.

"Tell us what else you did, Lia," her father urged. "You barely wrote at all the last few weeks."

Lia talked about the banquet and mentioned some of the activities. She told them about getting together with her cabinmates at Halloween. "It's all right if they come, isn't it?" Lia asked a little anxiously.

"Of course. It sounds like fun," Mrs. Greene said. "And by then, maybe you'll be able to introduce them to some of your friends here."

Lia rolled her eyes. Yeah right, she thought. How many times was she going to have to tell her mother not to get her hopes up?

Once she walked through the door, Lia was surprised at how happy she was to be home. The cloud around her lifted the moment her dog, a little white poodle named Flower, came running up to her, yipping and yapping.

"Hi, Flower. Hi, sweetie. Did you miss me?" She picked the dog up and held her close.

"She sure did miss you," Mr. Greene said. "She moped around here all summer."

Lia put Flower down. She looked around the living room. It was a lovely room with windows all around and all sorts of interesting nooks and crannies. The house was a Victorian, built at the turn of the century, and Mrs. Greene had decorated it with lots of antiques. But something was new here. "Mom, you changed the drapes."

"Not only down here," Mrs. Greene said, with a mischievous grin.

"You finally got me new curtains?" Lia asked with surprise.

"And a new bedspread."

Lia bounded up the stairs to her room. "You got the ones I picked out last spring," she squealed.

"You still like them, I hope," Mrs. Greene said.

"I sure do." Lia flopped down on the bed.

"Well, don't get the bedspread dirty quite yet," Mrs. Greene said with a frown.

Lia kicked off her shoes. "I guess I know I'm home now."

Her mother came over, sat down on the bed, and gave Lia a hug. "And I'm sure glad of that, sweetheart. So what would you like to do for the rest of the day?"

"Take a nap," Lia said promptly.

Mrs. Greene laughed. "That's reasonable, I suppose. I'm planning on making a special dinner. What would you like?"

Lia thought about it for a few seconds. Her mom made terrific fried chicken, but a barbeque would be fun, too.

"I think hamburgers on the grill. The hamburgers at camp tasted like shoe leather."

"All right. Shall we invite Scott and his family over?"

"Sure." Good old Scott. It would be nice to see a friendly face.

Even though the sun was now shining brightly, Lia climbed into her pajamas, pulled the covers up over her, and immediately fell asleep. By the time she woke up, it was almost six.

"Lia," her mother called from the doorway. "You'd better get up. The Tierneys will be here soon."

Lia bounded out of bed. "You should have got me up sooner."

"You were sleeping so peacefully, I didn't want to wake you."

Lia was still a little fuzzy from all that sleep, and her mother was wrong, it hadn't been all that peaceful. She'd kept having weird dreams. In one, she had been at a rock concert, wandering around trying to find someone she knew.

Lia headed into the bathroom and splashed water on her face. Her hair was a mess, so she fixed it into one long braid. Peering at her reflection, she noticed that being in the sun all summer had made her hair look even lighter. It looked pretty.

"Now, what am I going to wear?" she muttered. Her father had brought her trunk upstairs, but everything in it was wrinkled or worse. Lia went to her closet on the off chance there was something wearable hanging there. A pretty T-shirt with purple and pink flowers on a white background, one that Mrs. Greene had deemed too good for camp, was in the back of the closet. Gratefully, Lia grabbed it and figured she could wear it with an old pair of cutoffs that she had stuffed in her drawer.

By the time Lia smelled the charcoal burning, she was dressed and ready to go downstairs.

Mr. and Mrs. Tierney were sitting on chaise lounges drinking iced tea. "Hi Lia," Mrs. Tierney greeted her. "Welcome home."

"Thanks." She looked around.

"Scott will be here soon," Mr. Tierney said.

Lia felt embarrassed that it was so obvious she was looking for Scott.

"He's on the phone with Phil. Phil just got back from camp, too," Mrs. Tierney said.

"Here I am," Scott said, bounding around the corner. "Hi, Lia," he said cheerfully.

Lia had thought she might be shy when she first saw Scott, but her reaction was shock. "You grew!"

Scott laughed. "You noticed."

"It would be a little hard not to." Lia was sure that Scott had been at least an inch shorter than she was when the summer started. Now she was looking up at him. And that wasn't the only difference. Scott had always been a little funny looking, his nose and ears, in particular, taking up more room than they should. But now they seemed to fit much better. His hair was longer, too. *He's cute*, she thought with amazement.

"I have to buy Scott all new clothes," Mrs. Tierney said, taking a sip of her tea. "If I can get him to go shopping."

The mention of shopping turned Lia's thoughts away from Scott. "Boy, I wish someone would take me on a shopping spree." Lia turned to her mother. "Hint, hint."

"I don't think you've grown all that much," her mother said dryly. "But maybe we can pick out a couple of new things."

"Hey, I have a good idea," Scott suggested. "Mom, you take Lia shopping. That'll make everyone happy. You get to go on a buying spree, Lia gets clothes, and Mrs. Greene doesn't have to spend a penny. Oh, yeah, and I get out of the whole thing."

Everyone laughed.

"I think you ought to put your last reason first," Mrs. Tierney said.

"Forget it, Scott," her husband added. "When mothers want to take you shopping, there's not much you can do about it."

"No kidding." Scott said. "That's all right, maybe I'll just go shopping and I'll be the best-dressed kid in Maple Park. So, Lia," Scott said, turning to her. "How was camp? Tell me, and then I'll tell you about my summer. It was fun, too. My cousin was here and he taught me some magic tricks."

"Like what?"

"Oh, card tricks, and how to make a rope disappear."

Who made the old Scott disappear? Lisa wondered. *Some trick.*

THREE

Lia stood in front of her closet, just staring. Somehow, she thought that if she wore precisely the right outfit for her first day of school, maybe things would go better for her than they had last year.

It was kind of cool out, which was good. That way, she wouldn't have to wear some tired old thing she'd been wearing all summer. Her mother had taken her shopping after all, and she'd picked out a couple of sweaters, a pair of jeans, and a plaid flannel shirt. The shirt and jeans needed to go through the washer and dryer a couple of times to be really wearable. So Lia pulled out the new blue sweater with little white flowers embroidered on it. She could wear it with leggings.

When she was finally dressed to her satisfaction, her hair braided and rebraided, Lia went downstairs for breakfast. Her father had already gone to work. He worked at an electronics company where he did something with computers. Mrs. Greene worked for her brother, Lia's uncle Danny, who was a dentist. It wasn't much fun having an uncle as a dentist. He always told her she shouldn't be afraid of having work done on her teeth, because, after all, her dentist was her very own uncle who loved her. Lia could never quite tell him that when she was sitting in that chair with her mouth open, it didn't matter that the guy standing over her was her uncle. He still had a big, gleaming drill in his hand.

"Good morning, Lia," Mrs. Greene said, looking up from the newspaper. She took off her glasses. "Ready for the seventh grade?"

"I guess."

"How about a little more enthusiasm?"

Lia just sat down and poured herself a glass of orange juice.

"Do you want me to drive you to school?"

"No, Mom, I'll walk."

"Maybe you could stop for Missy."

"She'll be walking with Eden."

"So you'll both walk with Missy."

"Maybe," Lia answered noncommittally.

Mrs. Greene gave Lia one of her intense looks, but she didn't say anything more. Last week, she had insisted that Lia call one of the girls, so Lia had phoned Missy, who lived down the street.

Missy had been nice when Lia called, but had told her she had plans with Eden that afternoon. She didn't invite Lia along.

Lia had been relieved, but when she recounted the conversation to her mother, she had told it in a now-will-you-leave-me-alone tone of voice. Stopping for Missy was the first suggestion her mother had made in days. Maybe her mother was getting the picture.

Mrs. Greene went over to a drawer and pulled out her date book. "Lia, I made a doctor's appointment for you next week."

"Why?"

"It's time you had a checkup. And I made an appointment with Uncle Danny in three weeks."

"Oh, Mom, do I have to? I'm sure I don't have any cavities."

"Uncle Danny will be the judge of that."

Lia pouted. First day of school and the promise of upcoming doctor and dentist appointments. This morning was already a downer and it wasn't even nine o'clock. Then Lia had a thought.

"Am I going to see Uncle Danny in Evanston?"

Her mother nodded. "Saturdays and Tuesdays he's in the Evanston office." Mrs. Greene worked in his Maple Park office. "I didn't want to take you out of school for an appointment."

"Then can I see Jill when we go?"

"Jill? Oh, one of your friends from camp."

"I could go out to lunch with her," Lia said eagerly, "and then I could take the train back up here."

Mrs. Greene frowned. "You've never taken the train alone before."

"Mom, it's not that big a deal. I'll look at the train schedule. Jill would wait at the station with me."

"I suppose I could do some shopping and then drive you home," her mother said.

Lia would have preferred taking a train. That would have been more fun, but she knew better than to press her luck.

"I just want to see Jill. I don't really care how I get home."

Her mother looked like she was going to say something, but she hesitated.

Lia knew what was coming. *I should have known it was too good to last*, she thought.

"I . . . I don't mean to sound like a broken record, and I'm glad, really darling, that you enjoyed your camp friends so much. It's just that—"

Lia pushed aside her glass of juice. "Mom, don't."

Her mother sat down across the table from her. "I just hate to see you moping around."

"I haven't been moping," Lia said indignantly. "I've gone to the library, hung out with Scott. . ." Thank goodness for Scott. After Lia's initial reaction to the new Scott, she had been able to settle into their old friendship. Scott had gotten a lot of new stamps over the summer, and Lia's grandmother had been to Europe and sent her stamps from Italy, Switzerland, and Greece. Scott and Lia had spent several hot, lazy afternoons working on their collections. Every once in a while, as a break, they tried to teach their dogs how to catch a Frisbee. Without much success.

Mrs. Greene pushed her brown hair out of her eyes. "I'm overreacting. You're right."

"I am?" Lia asked with surprise. Her mother usually didn't back down that easily when she was on a roll.

"Look, you're starting school today. Go and have a good time. The last thing you need is to get all uptight about friends." She took a sip of her now cold coffee. "Scott's a start. And he's awfully cute. Don't you think he got cute over the summer?"

Lia picked up her books. She didn't know which was worse: having her mother bug her about her friends, or having her act like Scott was going to be her first boyfriend or something. "I'm going, Mom."

Her mother blew her a kiss. "Have a good day. Maybe we'll go out to dinner tonight and celebrate the new year."

Lia was happy when she walked out the door and a cool breeze hit her face. She felt free, even if she was on her way to school.

School was about six blocks away, too close for the bus, although when the winter winds were howling, she wouldn't have minded a big yellow bus pulling up on the corner. Sometimes her mother gave her a lift, but most of the time, Lia just walked.

The sound of pounding feet behind her made Lia turn around. Scott stopped short, before he could bump into her.

"I feel like I'm on my way to prison," he grumbled.

"Hello to you too."

"Sorry. But going back to school is such a bummer. I bet math's going to be really hard this year."

"You say that every year."

"And every year I'm right," Scott said triumphantly.

Math wasn't the best subject for either of them.

Lia had avoided talking about her social situation since she returned from camp, but she had complained about it plenty last year. She felt like complaining about it now. "Well, at least you have friends," Lia said, kicking at one of the first falling leaves.

"Thanks. What am I, chopped liver?"

"I didn't mean that," Lia told him. "It's just school would be more fun if I had a few girlfriends." She corrected herself. "I'd settle for one."

"What about all your pals from camp?" Lia had told him all about the Holiday Five.

Lia brightened. "Yeah, I think I might see Jill in a couple of weeks."

"Who knows? Maybe someone new will show up here that you can be friends with."

But by the end of the day, it was clear there were no new faces in the seventh grade at Field Elementary school. Lia had been panicked that she was going to have to sit alone at lunch, but she had screwed up her courage and sat with Eden and Missy and some of the other girls. No one had shooed her away, but Lia hadn't participated much in the conversation. Everyone was talking about what they had done all summer. Lia supposed she could have joined in, but what was she going to say? That she had come home with a trophy for all-around camper? Who was going to believe that?

By the time Lia got home, she was more than anxious to call Jill. She wanted to hear a friendly voice.

Lia settled herself with the phone in the den, glad that there was a note from her mother saying she wouldn't be home for another hour.

As she dialed Jill's number, Lia felt a flutter somewhere between her chest and her stomach. Would Jill be glad to hear from her? Or was she already so comfortable in her regular life that Lia would just be a distraction?

She was so nervous she dialed the wrong number. Checking the number in her address book once more, she dialed more slowly. This time Jill answered.

"Jill, it's Lia."

"Lia, hey. How ya doing?" Jill asked happily.

Lia felt relief flood her. "Fine. Fine as you can be after the first day of school."

"I've been back for a couple of days already. I'm looking at my homework piled up on my desk."

For a few moments they chatted about what they'd been doing since camp was over. Then Lia told Jill about her dentist appointment and her idea for lunch.

"Terrific!" Jill responded. "I'm glad I don't have to wait around until Halloween to see you."

"Me too, you," Lia responded. She told Jill where her uncle's office was located, and Jill said that it was near her ice-skating rink. She took lessons on Saturday morning.

"I want to take the train back."

"That shouldn't be a problem. They run every hour."

"You mean you've taken the train alone?" If Jill could do it, so could she.

"Well, only with my brother," Jill admitted.

Lia didn't think that would be an argument to sway her mother. "Where should we go for lunch?" Lia asked.

"Oh there's millions of places. Pizza, ribs, burgers, Chinese. Whatever we want."

"Great. Well, I'll call you a couple of days before my appointment and we'll fix a time and place to meet. I never thought I'd be so happy to be going to the dentist."

"I need you to open wider. What's the problem?" Uncle Danny asked, staring down at her with a frown.

What did he want her to say with a mouth full of cotton? Lia wondered. She tried to pull her chin down to her chest.

"Better," Uncle Danny said, coming at her with a gleaming instrument.

Lia tried to think of other things, not very easy with her uncle poking and prodding. She had had a cavity after all. At least the drilling part was over. Now she just had to try and ignore that squeaky sound as he pushed the silver goop into the cavity. When Lia was little, Uncle Danny had told her he was carving her initials into her tooth. Actually, it had only been a couple of years ago that she realized he was kidding.

"Okay," her uncle said, after several long moments. He took the wad of cotton out of her mouth and let her spit the excess silver into the small sink. "Done. Now, that didn't hurt, did it?"

Uncle Danny had the same hopeful expression Lia had seen on Flower's face when she wanted her supper.

"Not too bad," Lia finally said. She slipped off the chair, anxious to get to lunch.

Her uncle gave her a kiss on the top of her head. Then he reached into a drawer and handed her a new toothbrush. "Here, a present for you."

Lia laughed. "Mom brings these home all the time. We have a million of them."

Uncle Danny pretended to be surprised. "You mean your mother's been stealing toothbrushes from me? And a million of them, no less. I'm going to have to speak to her about that. Let's go."

Mrs. Greene was in Uncle Danny's office, doing some filing for him. He had told her when they came in that she didn't have to do any work. "Sit and read a magazine," he'd urged her. "You say you never have time to read."

His sister had looked at him as if he was mad. "Danny, you only have a part-time receptionist in this office. You probably have a desk full of folders that need to be filed."

Now, as they walked into his office, Lia could see that her mother had done more than a little filing. The place was practically gleaming. Even Uncle Danny's diplomas hanging on the wall looked as though they had been dusted.

"Did we hire a cleaning service?" Uncle Danny looked around in amazement.

"It was a mess. You've even got coffee stains on your new wooden desk. Danny, you've got to be more careful," she scolded.

Pretending Lia's mother wasn't there, Uncle Danny said to Lia, "You're lucky you don't have a big sister. They can be so bossy."

"So can mothers."

Mrs. Greene took the teasing good-naturedly. "Okay, okay, maybe I get a little carried away. But you're both lucky to have me. You'd probably get buried in junk if I wasn't around."

"Sounds like fun," Uncle Danny said. "Don't you think, Lia?"

Lia's mother swatted him.

"Nancy, you're right. We need you, we do," Uncle Danny agreed. "Now, I've got to get to my next patient." He gave them a wave.

Lia and her mother gathered their things. As they walked out the door, Mrs. Greene said in a troubled voice, "I don't know if I'm doing the right thing, Lia."

Lia knew exactly what she was talking about. Thanks to a plugged drain, she was going to get to take the train home after all. "Mom, we've been over this fifty times. You have to get back home for the plumber. I've got a train schedule. You showed me exactly where to stand on the platform. Jill is going to wait with me. What's the big deal?"

"I guess it isn't," her mother said uncertainly.

"I get on the train. I go five stops. I get off. Trust me, I can handle it."

Her mother looked at her, a little sadly. "You're growing up."

"Well, I will if you let me."

Mrs. Greene drove Lia to the pizza place where she was meeting Jill. "Do you want me to come in with you? What if Jill isn't there?"

For a moment, Lia panicked. What if Jill couldn't make it for some reason? Then she saw her standing in front of the restaurant. "It's okay. There she is."

"Where?" her mother asked.

"Right under the awning. In the red jacket."

For a second her mother looked surprised. Lia wondered why. Then it registered. She had never mentioned that Jill was African American. It hadn't seemed that important.

Her mother pulled into a parking space. "Is it all right if I come say hello?"

"Sure."

Mrs. Greene got out of the car and Lia introduced them. "I'm very glad to meet you."

"Nice to meet you, too," Jill said politely.

"I would have liked to meet all Lia's friends on Parents Day, but my husband and I couldn't make it up. We had to go to New York. My father-in-law was ill."

"Lia told me. I hope he's better now."

Mrs. Greene smiled at Jill. "Yes he is. Thank you for asking. Now, Jill, you do know where the train station is, don't you?"

"Sure." Jill seemed surprised at the question.

Mrs. Greene ignored Lia's glare. "Well, all right then. Lia, your dad will pick you up in Maple Park. Have fun, you two."

"Thanks," Jill said.

Walking into the restaurant, Lia said, "I'm surprised my mother didn't want to pin my name and address on my sweater in case I get lost. Is your mom like that?"

Jill shook her head. "I'm the youngest of three. Maybe she acted like that with my brother and sister, but she's lightened up now. My sister's always complaining that she's a lot easier on me."

The hostess showed them to a seat and handed them menus.

"I love the sausage pizza here," Jill said.

"Sounds great. Can we have mushrooms, too?"

"Sure," Jill said agreeably. They gave their order to the waitress who had appeared at their table.

"Have you talked to any of our fellow Holiday Fivers?" Jill asked.

"Kathy called. She wanted to know if we were wearing costumes for the Halloween stuff."

"Are we?"

"Yeah. Everyone wears a costume to the community center. Even some of the grown-ups."

"That's good. I thought maybe I'd worn my last Halloween costume," Jill said.

"I love dressing up," Lia confided.

"Me too. That's one of the things I like about skating. You get to wear all those spangles and crowns and it's cool."

The pizza arrived, and the girls dug in immediately.

"So who've you been hanging out with this year?"

Lia looked up at her, startled. "What?"

"Who are you friends with?"

Lia hesitated. She didn't know if she wanted to get into it. But Jill looked so concerned, so willing to listen that Lia's problems just began spilling out. She started at the beginning and told her how things had gone bad when Eden and her big ideas had arrived and that this year was shaping up the same way.

"I just don't fit in at all," Lia complained. "I wish I was back at camp."

Jill nodded. "I know how that is."

"You!"

"Oh, it's not that I don't have friends. I do. But some of my friends are white and some are black, and they don't always get along. Then there's the ice skating."

"I thought you loved it."

"I do. But I'm one of the only black kids who skate at my rink. Think about it. There weren't that many black kids at camp either. Sometimes I feel just like you do. That I don't fit in."

Lia leaned back in her seat. Jill always seemed so together. Lia had supposed that it was the poise that came with the ice skating. She was the last person Lia would have guessed felt out of place.

"Surprised you, huh?" Jill said, taking a sip of her cola.

Lia nodded. "But it makes sense. What do you do about it?"

"I just try to go with the flow. Like my mom says, 'Don't look for hassles and if they find you, step aside.' "

"Go with the flow, huh," Lia said thoughtfully.

"Should be easy for you, Lia. That's what you did at camp all summer. You just flowed right into all those activities. You never seemed uptight at all. And look what happened. You found four friends."

"Found them right in the beds next to me," Lia said with a giggle.

"That's true," Jill laughed along with her. "We were kind of in your face. But, heck, we didn't have to like you."

"I was worried you wouldn't," Lia admitted. "I guess I forgot to be so uptight when I went to camp."

Jill shrugged. "So there's your answer. Forget again. Everything's easier when you're not uptight."

FOUR

It sure was easy to go with the flow when Jill was around. The girls zipped through their pizza, leaving plenty of time to browse in some of the stores before train time. While they were in one of Evanston's many boutiques, Jill decided that Lia needed a whole new look.

"Oh, come on," Lia said. "I can't change the way I look. I'll probably look the same for the next fifty years."

"Fifty years of a braid! Girl, you *are* stuck in the mud. Let me wave my magic wand over you."

Lia looked at her watch. "I've got a half hour before I need to walk to the train. Let's see what kind of a magician you are."

Jill smiled broadly. "Okay. First, we lose the braid."

Lia pulled the rubber band from her hair and shook her hair free. Then she and Jill dashed around the store, picking up a couple of fancy dresses. Far too fancy for any occasion that Lia would be attending.

In the dressing room, Lia put on a deep blue velvet off-the-shoulder number, with a satin bow at the waist. Jill combed out Lia's hair so it curled long and loose.

"Now, the final touch." Jill pulled a lipstick out of her purse.

"You're allowed?"

"No way. It's my sister's." She put a generous amount on Lia's lips. She stood back to admire her handiwork. Then, she turned Lia around to look in the mirror. "Ta-da!"

"Wow!" Lia was impressed. "I'm going to cause a sensation when I walk into first-period English looking like this."

"Don't you think you should save it? Maybe for a festive occasion like lunch?" Jill deadpanned.

A saleswoman poked her head in the dressing room and looked at the girls questioningly. "Are you being helped?"

"Uh, we're fine," Jill said, trying to sound serious.

The saleswoman glanced at the expensive party

dresses hanging on the hooks. "Are your mothers with you?"

Lia and Jill exchanged glances. "No," Lia said.

"Not right now," Jill quickly added. "In fact, we've got to meet them. We don't have time to try on any more dresses."

"Then I'll just take these out of the dressing room if you don't mind."

"Oh, we don't mind," Jill said sweetly.

They burst into giggles as soon as she swept out of the room.

"We shouldn't have told her we were on our way to meet our mothers," Lia said.

"Why not? We are. Eventually."

Regretfully, Lia took off the dress and wiped the lipstick off with a tissue. She went to rebraid her hair but Jill said, "Leave it. It looks good."

Lia studied herself in the mirror. Why didn't she wear her hair down more often? It was just habit to braid it, she guessed. Well, she didn't have time to do it up now. Not with that saleslady waiting for them to vacate the dressing room.

Hurrying, Lia got herself together and she and Jill slunk out of the dressing room. Fortunately, the saleslady was off helping someone else.

"Too bad we don't have time to hit a few more stores," Jill said, looking at her watch.

"We're just going to make it as it is," Lia said, quickening her pace. "My mom will kill me if I miss that train. She probably won't let me go anywhere else by myself until I'm thirty."

Running the last few blocks, Lia and Jill huffed and puffed up the stairs and got to the platform just as the train was pulling into the station.

"Maple Park?" Lia double checked with the conductor. She didn't want to go the wrong way and end up in Chicago.

He nodded, and Lia headed into the car after a final wave at Jill.

Once she was settled, Lia felt like a real traveler, even if she was only going five stops. She was going alone.

As the train rolled by the pretty parks and houses, Lia thought about what fun she had had with Jill. Now it was back to boring old Maple Park.

Her father was waiting, as promised, at the train station. "So, you made it," Mr. Greene said, as he walked her over to the car. "I knew you could handle the trip. Each and every one of those five stops." He gave her a little wink.

Lia smiled up at her dad. Tall, balding a little, Mr. Greene was wearing his usual Saturday outfit, jeans and a sweatshirt. Her dad was more casual than her mother in the way he dressed and in the way he acted. He wasn't a worrier.

"Hey, your hair's down."

"Jill thought I should try it a new way." She decided not to mention the circumstances that had inspired Jill's suggestion.

"I like it. Did you have fun?" he asked, starting the car.

"Yes."

"More fun than you have around here, right?"

"Right." Her mood soured. It was easy to think things were going to change when she was having an afternoon with Jill, but what were the chances of that actually happening? "It'll probably be another month before I have any fun again."

"That sounds a little bleak," Mr. Greene said with a frown.

"It sure does. But Dad, I know all the girls in my class. And they're totally uninterested in me."

"These things go in waves, Lia. Before you know it, you'll be right in the middle of things again."

The next couple of days didn't do much to prove

her father right. During lunch, Lia continued to sit with the girls she had been friendly with before Eden arrived, just to prove to herself that she could do it. But the discussion only swirled around her. Since the girls were usually talking about what they had done together, there wasn't much room for her to slip into the conversation. Then, on Thursday, Eden started talking excitedly about Fortnightly.

Lia vaguely remembered hearing something about Fortnightly at the beginning of the semester. It was a new dance class for the sixth, seventh, and eighth graders that was going to be held every other Friday after school in the gym.

"It's going to start next week," Sarah added.

The girls talked about what they were going to wear.

"I think we should wear skirts or dresses," Eden said.

"I don't think I even own a dress," Frannie argued. "What's wrong with jeans?"

Eden shook her head. "Dancing in jeans is gross."

Eden's word was law, and even though Lia wasn't really part of the group, that didn't mean she could be a lawbreaker. She mentally went through her wardrobe. Did she have any skirts or dresses that would be appropriate for a dance class?

"So, what do you think, Lia?" Missy asked.

Lia was so surprised to hear her name, she nearly jumped. "Uh, dresses are good."

"We're done talking about that," Eden said impatiently. "I already decided. I asked you if Scott was going to come to Fortnightly."

"I don't know."

"But he lives next door to you, and you're friends, aren't you?" Eden persisted.

"Yes. But we've never talked about dance class."

"Well, try to find out," Eden ordered.

What was the big deal about Scott coming to Fortnightly? Lia wondered. Then it all made sense. She obviously wasn't the only one who had noticed the new Scott.

"Fortnightly would hardly be worth it if Scott wasn't there," Sarah commented.

As she walked home alone, Lia wondered how she could bring up Fortnightly. It wasn't the sort of topic they usually talked about. She was going to his house after school, and she supposed they'd discuss what they usually did — stamps.

Scott's uncle was doing business in Asia, and he was sending Scott stamps from Hong Kong, Thailand, and China. Scott was sitting in his family room sorting his latest batch when Lia walked in, MTV blaring in the background.

"Let me see what you've got," Lia demanded, without even a hello.

They spent the next half hour looking over the new stamps, until, right out of the blue, Scott asked, "So what about this Fortnightly thing?"

Lia was both surprised and relieved. At least she wasn't going to have to bring it up. "What about it?"

"Are you going?"

"I guess," Lia replied. "Are you?"

Scott shrugged.

"Is that a yes or no?"

"I think my mother is going to make me. She heard about it at a PTA meeting last night, and she came home all excited. Not only will I learn to dance, but now she's got a reason to buy me more new clothes."

Lia leaned back against the couch. "I think we need to trade mothers."

"What are the girls saying about Fortnightly?" Scott asked, suddenly very interested in putting his stamps in their clear, plastic envelopes. He didn't look at Lia at all.

"Most of the girls are excited about it. What about the boys?"

"Some of them are pretty interested. Others don't

want to go anywhere near the gym. Phil says the gym is for playing basketball, not dancing. He swears he's not going.

"So if he's not going, I hope you are."

"Me?" Lia squeaked.

"Well, I want someone to hang out with. Besides, you being there is even better than Phil."

"Why?"

"Because I can dance with you."

Lia was surprised to feel her heart start to beat a little faster. "You want to dance with me?"

"Well, sure. If I step on your feet, we'll just laugh about it. I step on Eden's or Missy's toes, and they'll probably get all snooty."

Lia laughed with nervous relief. She had thought Scott was about to go mushy on her. "I'm not all that anxious to dance with some of the boys, either. Tim Carver probably has sweaty palms."

"Hey," Scott exclaimed, "I've got a great idea."

"What's that?"

"Let's just dance with each other. That way, I won't have to worry about stomping on anyone."

"And I won't have to worry that no one will ask me to dance," Lia said thoughtfully.

"So then it's a deal? We just dance with each

other?" Scott's expression was hopeful. Like a dog about to get a treat.

"Why not?"

Scott put out his hand. Lia shook it. She noticed that it wasn't sweaty at all.

The next day at lunch, Lia felt like she finally had a reason to be sitting with the girls. Although she didn't mention the pact she had made with Scott, just being able to offer the news that he was coming to Fortnightly seemed to raise Lia's stock.

"He's coming? That's great," Eden said with satisfaction.

"You're so lucky," Missy said. "You get to hang out with him all the time."

"We're just friends," Lia protested.

"Really?" Frannie asked skeptically.

"He's my next-door neighbor. We go over our stamp collections together."

"Maybe I could collect stamps," Eden said thoughtfully. "How do you start?"

Lia had to smile. Eden was more likely to collect earrings or posters of rock stars than stamps.

Eden caught Lia's smile, but instead of being angry, she started to laugh. "Okay, so I don't really want to do the stamp thing. What else does Scott like?"

"His dog. Sports. Hamburgers."

"So far, hamburgers are the only thing we have in common," Eden said.

The conversation moved to their English assignment, and then to a TV show most of the girls had watched the night before. Lia had missed it, but it didn't seem to matter. For once she didn't have to try to be a part of things. She just was.

Putting on a dress for school felt absolutely weird. Eden, whose father was a doctor, probably had a dozen dresses in her closet, just on the off chance she wanted to wear one. Lia had two, one that she had worn to her cousin's wedding last spring, and one that her mother had bought her when she found out the girls were going to dress up for Fortnightly.

Lia had told her mother over the weekend about Eden's dress edict. To her surprise, Mrs. Greene had been delighted.

"But Mom, when we went shopping before school started, you were complaining about all the money you were spending on clothes for me. I didn't think you'd want to buy me anything else."

Mrs. Greene put down the book she was reading. "But this is a dress!" she said enthusiastically.

Lia sat down beside her on the living room couch. "So?"

"You never wear dresses. And you look so pretty in them. When you were a little girl I loved dressing you up," Mrs. Greene said nostalgically. "Remember that white cotton dress you had, with the pink-and-white piping? You looked like a little doll in it."

Lia rolled her eyes. She had been four when she wore that dress. She only remembered it because her mother had about a million pictures of her in it.

Mrs. Greene tossed her book on the coffee table. "So let's go."

"Where?"

"Shopping of course."

"Now?"

"No time like the present," Mrs. Greene said happily.

So off they had gone to the mall. Lia liked shopping, but even she was getting grouchy by the time two hours had gone by and they hadn't found anything they could agree on. The dresses her mother kept oohing and aahing over weren't that different from the dress she had tried on in the boutique. Her mother seemed particularly fond of velvet.

"Mom, Fortnightly is going to be held in the gym. I'll come home dressed in purple velvet and sweat from the last basketball game."

"I just want you to look nice," her mother said in a hurt voice.

"I will look nice," Lia countered irritably, "in a dress that I pick out."

Finally, they compromised on a flowered dress with short sleeves. She liked the way it made her look. Like she almost had a figure.

At least, she thought it looked cute in the store. Here, standing in front of her mirror, wearing the dress, her hair flowing around her shoulders, Lia looked so different from her normal self, she couldn't tell whether she looked terrific or terrible. She wished she could just change back into her regular old clothes, but then she'd really look out of place. She either had to wear the dress or not go at all.

"You look great," she told herself firmly.

She just hoped everyone else thought so.

FIVE

Mr. Crocker stood with his arms folded. The gym teacher had the same stern expression on his face that Lia had seen in the first grade when she had trouble turning a somersault.

"What's he doing here?" Lia whispered to Missy, who was standing next to her hugging the wall of the gym. The girls were all clustered together, as were the boys. No one had directed them to group that way. It just seemed natural. "I thought Miss Nestor was going to be in charge."

Before Missy could answer, Mr. Crocker clapped his hands together just the way he did when he wanted to get teams together for medicine ball.

"I suppose you all know why you're here. You're going to learn to dance."

"Sounds fun so far," Lia muttered.

"Miss Nestor will be your dancing teacher. I've agreed to help out. I'll be her dancing partner." He glared at the assembled group as if daring them to let loose with one snicker.

Miss Nestor hurried into the gym. "Sorry I'm late. I'm sure we're all excited about being here." Miss Nestor was one of the most popular teachers in the school. In her late twenties, she had only been teaching for a couple of years. Quick and pretty, with long red hair that she wore pulled back with a variety of barrettes, she taught music to the upper grades. Half the boys in the gym had a crush on her.

"Let me tell you how this is going to work," she continued. "We'll start out with a dance step. Mr. Crocker and I will demonstrate." She turned her sunshine-bright smile on the gym teacher and her glow softened him. He nodded at her agreeably. "Then," she continued, "you'll try the steps yourselves with a partner. Don't look so worried. It will be fun."

Lia wondered exactly how those partners were going to be chosen. What if they got assigned partners and her deal with Scott was ruined? Her eyes darted over to the group of boys huddled together. Dancing with Scott was one thing. What if she got stuck with Pete Walters? He could barely walk to the pencil sharpener without tripping over his own feet. Dancing would take a quantum leap.

"The first thing we're going to show you is the box step. I know, I know," Miss Nestor said, responding to a couple of groans. "It sounds kind of boring. But it's the foundation for all slow dancing. So Mr. Crocker and I will start with that. When you begin dancing, we'll walk around the floor to see how you're doing."

The school hadn't sprung for a CD player, Lia noticed. Instead, an old phonograph had been found. Miss Nestor put the needle on the record. "I hope you like this song. It's a golden oldie from the fifties called 'Mr. Blue.' "

Lia was much less interested in the song than she was in watching Mr. Crocker put his arm around Miss Nestor's waist and tentatively pick up her hand. Even for a gym teacher, Mr. Crocker had a lot of muscles. You could see them rippling through his shirt. Lia wondered how it would feel to have a muscled arm around her waist. She looked around. She'd never find out with this group.

Lia thought Mr. Crocker might be kind of a clunky

dancer, but to her surprise, he was light on his feet, gliding with Miss Nestor around the room as she described what their feet were doing.

When they were done, Miss Nestor turned to the assembled group and said, "We're going to choose partners in different ways, but we'll start by alternating men's and ladies' choice. Guys, you can go first. Pick your partners."

There was a mad scramble. Even Eden looked nervous, Lia noticed as the boys galloped around choosing girls. Lia, however, was calm. She just turned around and there was Scott.

"Boy, I'm glad I made it over here in time," Scott said with relief.

"I don't think you were going to have to push guys out of the way to get to me," Lia remarked dryly.

"Pete Walters told me he was going to ask you."

For the first time, Lia realized how really happy she was to have a permanent partner. She looked around to see who Pete had ended up with. A few couples away, there was Pete standing with his arm stiffly around Eden, who looked as if she had swallowed a sour plum.

Smiling brightly at Scott, Lia took his hand, and they started to move to the music. Stepping on each

other's toes wasn't a problem because they kept
their heads bent, staring at their feet. That caused a
different problem, though—they bumped their heads.
Twice.

The second time, Lia thought she heard Scott mur-
mur something.

"Are you calling me a butthead?" she asked indignantly.

"No, I said, 'Stop butting my head.' "

Lia wasn't sure which was worse. "You bumped
me."

They looked at each other and burst out laughing.

"Dancing's hard enough without fighting," Scott
commented.

Lia didn't think it was so hard. She kind of liked it.

When the song was over, Miss Nestor said, "Now
that we've gotten a start, we're going to change partners, and try it again. This time the girls get to pick."

There was a buzz as the girls left the boys they had
been dancing with and hustled off to find new ones.
Only Lia and Scott stayed standing together.

Missy ran up to Scott. Then she glanced at Lia.
"Didn't you two just dance together?"

"I asked him this time," Lia replied.

Missy frowned and looked like she wanted to say

something more, but realizing her chance to find a halfway decent boy was fading, she darted away.

"I'm glad I didn't have to dance with her," Scott commented.

"What's wrong with Missy?" Lia asked with surprise.

"She's too . . . too talky."

Missy did talk a lot. But she was so pretty. Lia had thought that was all boys cared about.

Miss Nestor put on another song, called "Blue Velvet."

"I wish she'd get another color," Scott said as he tripped a little. "I'm not doing so hot with blue songs."

"Oh, you're doing great, Scott," Lia protested. "Just don't concentrate so hard."

"What else can I concentrate on?"

"Have you taught Skip how to catch a Frisbee yet?"

Scott shook his head. "He waits until it falls and then goes over and licks it like it's dinner."

"He'll learn."

"Probably faster than me learning this box step."

"Take a look around. *Some* people look like they're doing the triangle."

Scott nodded, but he looked relieved when the dance was over.

"I think we'll have a snowball now. Do you know what a snowball is?" Miss Nestor asked.

Some of the eighth graders did. Miss Nestor explained that two people began dancing, while the others stood in a circle. Then, when the music was interrupted, that couple picked two other people to dance with and so on, until everyone was dancing, except a few left-over girls.

"Who's going to start off?" one of the girls called.

"Well, Mr. Crocker and I will, if someone'll volunteer to work the record player."

About five boys raised their hands.

Miss Nestor picked one and put on a record. Then she and Mr. Crocker started dancing. When the music stopped, they went to pick other partners. Lia prayed Mr. Crocker wouldn't pick her. The thought of dancing with a man who wasn't her father was worse than the thought of tripping over Pete Walters. She needn't have worried. Mr. Crocker went straight to Jamie Jones, the tallest and most athletic of the eighth-grade girls.

Eden was the first of the girls in the seventh grade to be picked.

That figures, Lia thought. When it was time to snowball, Eden picked Scott, but they didn't dance very long before the music halted and Scott made a beeline for Lia. "Isn't it about time for this Fortnightly thing to be over?" he grumbled.

"Gee, thanks."

"I didn't mean anything personal, but I'm about danced out."

The music stopped. Lia looked around. There weren't that many boys left. One of the shyest kids in her class, Cliff Wallenberg, was looking at the ceiling. Lia went over to him, and he looked surprised and pleased when she took his hand.

When the snowball ended, Miss Nestor said, "I think that's about all we have time for today. We'll meet again in two weeks to practice what we've learned today and start the cha-cha."

"Does anybody do the cha-cha anymore?" Scott asked Lia as they left the school to walk home.

"I have a feeling by the time we're done with Fortnightly, we're going to be experts in a lot of dances no one does anymore," Lia replied.

"So how was the dancing?" Mrs. Greene asked, as soon as Lia walked into the kitchen.

"Fine."

"Did you dance with a lot of different boys?"

"Nope." She opened the refrigerator and took out a can of cola.

Mrs. Greene stopped chopping the vegetables for salad. "No one asked you to dance?"

"Scott and I made a deal to just dance with each other."

"Do you think that's a good idea?"

"Why isn't it?" Lia asked with surprise.

"I don't know. It just seems like it would be more fun to dance with a lot of different people."

Lia shook her head. "It wouldn't."

Her mother opened her mouth as if she was going to say more, but the phone rang.

Lia got it and was pleased to hear Jill's voice on the other end.

"Hey," Jill said, "how are you doing?"

"I'm tired," Lia replied. She explained about Fortnightly.

"Was it fun?" Jill asked.

Lia pondered that question for a moment. "I guess. I didn't hate it."

Jill's laugh bubbled over the wire. "What a recommendation."

"So what's going on?"

"I'm in a skating exhibition tomorrow at my rink. I thought you might like to come."

"Sounds great." Lia conferred with her mother, who said either she or Mr. Greene would take Lia to Evanston. "I can go," she reported back.

Jill told her what time to be there and gave her the location of the rink.

"See you there," Lia said gaily.

The next day Lia woke up in a good mood. The exhibition was at eleven, so she had a couple of hours to kill before it was time to leave. She decided to give Erin a call. She hadn't talked to her since they'd been back from camp.

"Lia!" Erin squealed, when she heard her friend's voice. "How are you? Are we still on for Halloween?"

"For sure. The party at the community center this year is going to be bigger than ever."

Lia got comfortable on her bed, the Mickey Mouse phone she had received for her last birthday cradled against her ear, and described the events she had read about in the flyer that had come in the mail yesterday from the park district.

"What kind of costumes do we need?" Erin asked.

"Well, you can wear anything you want, but I had an idea. Let me run it by you."

Lia had been up in the attic last week where her mother had been looking for some old photo albums. There had been trunks of old clothes up there. When she asked her mother what they were, Mrs. Greene had sighed.

"Remember when Grandma sold her house last spring? She found all these old clothes that belonged to her, and her mother, even a few things from her grandmother. She didn't want to throw them out, so she asked if I would keep them. Of course, I said yes, but frankly, I don't know what to do with them either."

Lia had spent a few moments looking through the trunks. There were all kinds of wonderful things, dresses with spangles and blouses with lace.

"There's some real vintage clothes there," Lia told Erin, after she explained about the trunks. "I thought we could put together costumes out of what we find."

"I can't wait to see them!" Erin exclaimed. "I was afraid I was going to have to go as a hobo. I just put on a bunch of torn old stuff the last time I went trick-or-treating."

"This will be much more elegant," Lia assured her. Lia told Erin about her lunch with Jill and going to the rink later. "I'll tell her about the costumes when I see her. Then I'll call the other girls."

"Say hi for me," Erin said. "Tell Jill I'm really looking forward to Halloween."

Since she had a little more time, Lia went to the hardware store with her father. When she came back, her mother said, "Eden called."

"She did?" Lia asked with surprise. "What did she want?"

"Call her back and find out."

Lia looked at the clock. "I don't have time now."

"It will only take a couple of minutes," her mother protested.

Lia looked at her mother curiously. "What's the big deal if I call now or when I get back?"

Mrs. Greene shrugged. "No big deal, I guess. But it's been such a long time since one of your friends from around here called . . ."

Now it was clear. Her mother wanted Lia to get back to Eden before a potential pal got away.

"Mom, Eden will be there when I get back. She probably wants to know what page our math homework's on."

"It's a start," Mrs. Greene muttered.

That got Lia mad. She stomped upstairs and stayed

there until it was time to leave for Evanston. Mr. Greene was going to take her. He wanted to go to the library there anyway.

Lia grumbled all the way to Evanston. "Why won't Mom get off my back with this friends thing? She's driving me crazy."

"Oh, Lia, she just wants you to have fun."

"I am having fun. I'm going to see Jill skate."

"You know what I mean. At home."

"But Mom acts like Eden is some big fish who's gonna swim away if I don't reel her in."

Lia and her father looked at each other and burst out laughing. Eden did look kind of like a fish. Her eyes were a little far apart, and her chin receded just a bit.

"Are you good at fishing?" Mr. Greene asked.

"I don't even care about fishing," Lia responded.

"Lia," Dad said more seriously, "I know your mom is worried, but I think you're handling this much better than you did last year. You're making real progress."

Shyly, Lia glanced over at her father. "I think I am, too."

It had crept up on her really. Between being with Scott, sitting with the girls at lunch, and anticipating her Holiday Five reunion, things didn't seem nearly so dismal as they had before she went away to camp.

Her dad dropped her off at the rink and told her to walk over to the library when she was done.

Lia had only been to an indoor rink a couple of times for birthday parties. She didn't really like skating, since she fell more than she stood, but she certainly admired anyone who could surf the ice, and she was eager to watch Jill.

There were a few minutes before the exhibition started. Lia walked past the deserted snack bar and into the rink. She hoped she'd have a chance to say hello to Jill before things got underway. Sure enough, Jill saw her and waved as soon as she took her seat in the front row. The stands were only half full, and Lia wondered if any of the other spectators were Jill's friends.

Jill skated over and landed at the rail with a flourish. "Hey, I'm glad you could make it."

"Me too. Are you nervous?"

"Not really. This is just a little show-off stuff for some of my teacher's students. He wants us to get practice skating in front of people. We started doing these routines last year, so he thinks we're ready for an audience."

"Do you feel ready?" Lia asked.

Jill shook her head. "I feel rusty. Everyone else kept up over the summer."

"You'll do great," Lia said loyally. "Are any of your school friends here?"

Jill shook her head. "I asked a couple, but none of them could come. My brother said he'd be here, though."

"Oh. Introduce me later." Why did Jill suddenly look embarrassed? Lia wondered.

"I'd better get back to the other kids," Jill said. Gracefully, she skated away.

Lia looked around the rink. It wasn't huge like the rinks on television, and the skaters weren't wearing glitzy costumes. Jill was dressed in a red-and-white shorts outfit with red tights. But there was still an excitement in the air.

The first skater up was a boy a little older than Jill, dressed in black slacks, a black vest and a white shirt. He nodded to the man running the sound system and proceeded to do his routine to a classical piece Lia didn't know the name of.

His movements were fluid, but even Lia could see that his technique wasn't that great. His leg shook when he lifted it high in the air, and his twirls were awfully wobbly.

The next girl was much better, but to Lia's eye, it didn't look as if the moves she was doing were very difficult. Then it was Jill's turn, and right away, Lia could see that Jill had something that the others didn't—a real presence. She smiled at the audience with such genuine enthusiasm while she was skating that she made everyone in the audience feel the excitement.

Lia could barely sit through the next girl's routine, she was so eager to find Jill and tell her what a great job she had done. When it was over, she hurried over to Jill, who was changing into her street shoes.

"You were wonderful!"

"Really?" Jill asked, a worried look on her face. "I wobbled so much on my spin."

"I didn't notice," Lia said honestly.

"My coach did," Jill replied ruefully. "I'll be practicing that move all next week."

Before Lia could reply, a tall teenager came over to them who looked so much like Jill it was obvious they were related.

"Hey, Jill, you were looking good out there."

"Thanks. Lia, this is my brother, Owen."

"Hi," Owen said gruffly.

"Hello." Owen didn't seem very friendly.

"Do you want to get a Coke or something?" Jill asked Lia. "We could all go."

Lia thought about it. Going out wasn't in the time frame she had given her father. He might start to worry if she took too long. "I don't think I'd better. I'm meeting my dad at the library."

"Oh, that's too bad," Jill said, but she sounded relieved.

"Well, I guess I'd better get going," Lia said uncertainly.

"All right. I'll talk to you before we come for Halloween."

Lia felt dismissed. She said good-bye and headed outside, but before she got to the door, she realized she wasn't exactly sure how to find the library. Oh well, Jill could tell her. Lia hurried back inside. Before she could turn the corner, she heard Jill and Owen coming down the hall, talking.

"Lay off me, Owen," Jill was saying in an angry voice.

"I just don't get it, sister. Why do you want to be hanging out with white girls all the time?"

*J*IX

Lia ducked into the ladies' room, praying that Jill wouldn't stop in there herself.

Holding her breath, she listened as Jill and Owen passed by. She could hear their voices, but she couldn't make out the words. Too bad. Lia would have liked to hear Jill's answer.

When she thought the coast was clear, Lia slipped out of the bathroom. A mother with a small child was passing by, and Lia asked the woman for directions to the library. She practically ran all the way there.

Mr. Greene was sitting at a table in the reading room, surrounded by several open books. Looking up, he saw Lia with her red face, and his expression became concerned. "Are you all right?"

"Yes," Lia answered, breathing heavily. "I was just walking fast."

"You didn't have to hurry," Mr. Greene said. "I wasn't going anywhere."

"I thought it would be rude to make you wait," Lia replied grumpily. "Excuse me."

Mr. Greene gave Lia a strange look, but he gathered his books and merely said, "I'm going to check these out."

On the way home, Lia sat silently in the front seat, thinking. When her father asked her how the exhibition was, she answered, "Fine," and didn't offer any details.

Lia was still smarting over Owen's remark. What was wrong with hanging around with white people? And what did Owen know about her and Jill's friendship, anyway?

It was true that Lia had never really had another friend who was black, but that was because there were so few in her class, and most of them were boys anyway. Or was that the reason? There had been one girl, Jasmine King, who had been in her class since kindergarten. She was gone this year, and Lia had heard she'd moved. Jasmine was nice enough, but she and Lia had never really spoken much. Now, Lia wondered why.

Lia had intended to go over and see what Scott was up to, but her mother, after asking about her afternoon and receiving the same curt reply Lia had given her father, told her that Eden had phoned again and wanted Lia to call as soon as she got home.

"She called again?" Lia asked with surprise. Eden couldn't want her math homework that much. Lia decided that she'd better find out what was so urgent.

The last thing Lia expected was an invitation to a sleepover, but that's what she got.

"Tonight?" Lia said doubtfully.

"Do you have plans?"

Was Eden saying that just to be snide? "Not exactly," Lia finally conceded.

"Then, why don't you come? Missy will be here too. We'll get pizza and rent a movie."

It seemed rude to say no when she didn't really have a reason to. Maybe it wouldn't be the most fun in the world, but it beat staying home watching television with her parents. Suddenly, Lia wanted very much to get out of the house on a Saturday night. "I guess I can make it."

"Do you have to ask your mom?" Eden asked into the silence.

Lia almost laughed. Her mother would probably be

dancing on the kitchen table when she found out Lia had an invitation for a sleepover. "I'm sure it will be okay."

Lia was right. "What time do you have to be there?" her mother asked with a big smile. "Are you having dinner with the girls?"

"We'll eat something, I guess," Lia sighed at her mother's enthusiasm. "I'm supposed to go over about eight."

Promptly at eight, Lia rang the doorbell to Eden's house.

Eden let her in, and Lia looked around curiously. She had never been to Eden's house. It was completely different from hers, ultra modern, with furnishings that were all chrome and glass and black leather. It all looked sleek, if not very comfortable.

"Is Missy here?" Lia asked as she stowed her backpack in the closet.

Before Eden could answer, the doorbell rang. "She's here now," Eden said.

The evening passed pleasantly enough. They ordered out for pizza and watched the comedy that Eden had rented. They even laughed at the same parts. In some ways it reminded her of being at camp.

It wasn't until the girls were in their pajamas and

getting settled in their sleeping bags in the family room that Lia got an inkling of the real reason she was there.

The light had just been turned off, and Lia was yawning when Eden rolled over and casually asked, "So are you and Scott going together now?"

"I already told you, no," Lia said sleepily.

"But you danced every dance together," Missy reminded her.

"We just wanted to."

"Because you like each other," Eden insisted.

Lia could tell that she wasn't going to get to sleep until she got this straightened out. "We're friends. We've been friends forever. We just thought instead of letting a bunch of different people step on our feet, we'd dance together and step on each other's."

Eden and Missy digested this. Then Eden spoke up. "But Lia, don't you realize what you're doing?"

I am not getting to sleep, she thought to herself, but out loud, she said, "No, what?"

"You're keeping Scott from dancing with all the other girls at Fortnightly."

"That's the idea."

"Well, it's a bad one," Eden said crossly.

Lia sat up and turned on the light. "What do you

want me to do about it? This was Scott's idea, not mine."

"Lia," Missy began earnestly, "there might be girls who really want to dance with Scott."

It all became clear. "You mean girls like you two."

"Oh, not me," Eden said importantly. "It's Missy that's got a crush on Scott."

"Eden!" Missy shrieked in embarrassment. "You said you wouldn't tell."

"Hey, I'm not stupid, Missy. I would have figured it out." Lia also had guessed why Eden had chosen not to set her sights on Scott. Last year, when he had been a shrimp with a bad haircut, Eden had either ignored him or disdainfully called him Scott the Dot. Eden was smart enough to know Scott wouldn't want her as his first girlfriend. Besides, Eden liked being a power behind the scenes. Lia suspected Eden would have more fun fixing up Missy and Scott than she would actually being with Scott herself.

Lia felt a little sorry for Missy, however. She really did look humiliated. "I can't get involved in Scott's private stuff," Lia said more gently.

"But you don't have to dance every dance with him," Eden insisted. "And what would be the harm in just telling Scott how nice Missy is?"

Was that a net Lia felt closing in around her?

"It's okay, Lia," Missy broke in. "You don't have to say anything."

Eden angrily turned to Missy. "What do you mean? That's the whole plan."

"Forget it. I don't want to go through with it anymore."

"Yes you do," Eden insisted. "All you do is talk about how much you like Scott."

Lia glanced at the clock. It was already midnight. She was getting awfully tired. She glanced over at Missy's downcast face. "But I guess I could say something about Missy," she conceded.

Missy immediately perked up. "What?"

"I don't know, just that you're fun or something."

"Well, it's a start," Eden muttered.

"Can we turn the light off now?" Lia asked. Reluctantly, looking as if she'd like to talk more, Eden obliged.

Now why had she said that? Lia wondered. How was she going to bring Missy's name into the conversation without being obvious? As she drifted off, Lia went over the events of the day. Having friends was awfully complicated.

The next morning, Eden seemed to feel that Lia

was the number one supporter of the Missy and Scott plan. Lia needn't have bothered worrying about what to tell Scott. Eden was full of ideas. She chattered on at breakfast about what exactly Lia could say about Missy and when.

"Like, if you're walking your dogs, you know," Eden said, forgetting to close her mouth while she chewed, "you could say that Missy is frightened of dogs, and wouldn't it be nice to invite her over so he could personally help her overcome her fears."

Missy quashed that one. "I'm not afraid of dogs."

Eden shrugged. "Scott doesn't know that. But all right, forget the dogs. What about if you tell him that Missy needs help with her math or something."

"You've just named Scott's worst subject," Lia informed her.

"All right. Just have Missy over and then the three of you can talk about anything you want."

"Look, I'm not promising anything," Lia said, regretting she had agreed to even bring up Missy's name. It would have been all right to have Missy over under normal circumstances, but this was hardly normal.

Eden patted her on the shoulder. "Don't worry. You'll do great."

With those words ringing in her ears, Lia went

home. The first person she saw when she got out of the car was Scott.

"Boy, you look bad," he commented.

Lia didn't even bother to argue. She had tossed and turned all night. "I know."

"What's the problem?"

You, among others, Lia wanted to inform him, but she didn't think she should do that. It wouldn't help Missy's plan if she spilled the beans two seconds after she saw him.

"Do you want to ride bikes this afternoon?"

"I'm too tired. I slept over at Eden's."

"Eden?" Scott made a face.

For some reason, this riled her. "Haven't you ever heard that beggars can't be choosers?"

"Whoa, don't jump all over me."

"Sorry," Lia said, immediately contrite.

"That's okay," Scott said easily. "If I'd spent an evening with Eden, I'd be in a bad mood, too."

"Missy was there," Lia added cautiously.

"Oh yeah? Say, if you don't want to ride bikes, maybe you can come over later and we can watch the Bears."

Both Lia and Scott were big Bears fans.

"Okay. That sounds like fun."

Later, after a brief nap, when Lia went over to Scott's and settled in his living room, she made her first attempt at Operation Missy. The game hadn't even started when she said. "The sleepover was kind of fun. I mean Eden can be a pain, but Missy's nice."

Scott took another handful of popcorn.

"Don't you think she's nice?" Lia persisted.

"Who?"

"Missy," Lia said impatiently. This was going to be even harder than she thought. She's nice, right?"

"Sure. She's okay."

After that, Lia was stumped. No matter how hard she tried to come up with another way to inject Missy's name into the conversation, she couldn't think of one. But that didn't stop her the rest of the week. When Missy gave an oral report, Lia made a point of telling Scott how good she thought it was. When Missy's team won in volleyball, she informed Scott. The response was the same as it had been on Sunday. If a bowl of popcorn had been handy, Scott would have taken a handful.

Meanwhile, Eden was eager to know how Lia was progressing. When Lia reported her lack of progress, Eden said maybe she wasn't trying hard enough.

"Why don't you try it then," Lia retorted.

The person who didn't ask any questions was Missy. When Eden queried Lia in front of her, Missy looked as if she wished she were somewhere else.

Finally, one day in the library, Lia pulled Missy aside. "How come you always look so weird when Scott's name comes up?"

"I don't want Scott to know I have a crush on him," she burst out. "And he's going to figure something is up if you keep talking about me."

"I thought I was doing what you wanted," Lia said, bewildered.

"What Eden wanted," Missy corrected. "I just want Scott to notice me on his own."

Lia didn't think that was going to happen. "So, should I lay off?"

"Please," Missy answered.

"Okay," Lia responded, trying to hide her relief.

Missy smiled at her. "Thanks. I should have just said something earlier, but I was embarrassed."

"Maybe you can ask him for a ladies' choice at Fortnightly."

"Maybe he'll ask me to dance," Missy said hopefully.

Lia's answer was careful. "Well, I'll tell him he doesn't have to stick to our deal if he doesn't want to."

But when Lia brought it up to Scott on their way to Fortnightly, Scott said, "No way. I like things just the way we did it last time." He looked at her suspiciously. "Is there somebody you want to dance with?"

"Not me."

So within a short time, Scott and Lia were back in the gym, which was now decorated for Halloween, doing the cha-cha.

"One, two, cha-cha-cha," Scott counted out loud as he tried to force his feet in the right direction. His counting was off. He only cha-chaed when he should have cha-cha-chaed.

Scott was relieved when the next ladies' choice was a slow dance. "At least we're back to something I almost know," he said as he put his arm around Lia's waist.

"You'll get the cha-cha," Lia consoled him.

"I'd rather be playing football."

Today Miss Nestor and Mr. Crocker had come up with some innovative ways for partners to be chosen for each dance. The next time, instead of the boys choosing, the girls got in one circle, the boys in a circle outside them. They marched around each other until the music stopped. Then they danced with the person next to them.

Lia found herself dancing the cha-cha with one of the eighth-grade boys. She didn't even know his name. Feeling shy, she kept her head down looking at her feet, but the boy said, "You don't have to do that. I saw you dancing with that kid you're always with. You're pretty good. He stinks."

"He does not," Lia said indignantly.

"What is he? Your boyfriend?"

"No."

"All I'm saying is you deserve a better partner." He gave her a crooked smile.

Lia was relieved when the dance was over and she could get back to Scott. But Miss Nestor called for a ladies' choice, and before she could get to Scott, another girl had already grabbed him. Lia looked around for someone she could ask to dance, but the only one in proximity was the eighth-grader she had just gotten rid of. She would have liked to just slink off to the ladies' room, but it seemed awfully rude.

"Would you like to dance?" she muttered.

"Couldn't stay away, huh?"

Lia just gritted her teeth and danced.

"You're not being very friendly."

Lia didn't like his attitude, but she wasn't very good at snappy replies. She didn't like it, either, when his arm tightened around her waist. Without saying anything, she pulled away.

When the dance was over and she finally got back to Scott, Lia said, "You're right. Even I'd rather be playing football."

"Let's get out of here," Scott said.

"You're kidding," Lia replied, startled.

"There's no law that says we have to stay for the whole thing," Scott pointed out.

"But if we just walk out, everyone will notice."

"If we walk out. But maybe not if we dance out?"

"Dance out?"

Scott put his arm around her, and slowly circled Lia toward the gym doors.

"Are you sure we ought to do this?" Lia whispered frantically.

"What are they going to do, put us in Fortnightly prison?" Scott answered back. "I tell you, not one person here knows whether we're here or not." With one final whirl, he headed toward the exit, and danced them out the door.

SEVEN

Scott was wrong. Everybody *did* notice that he and Lia had left. A couple of kids saw them dance out of the gym. Others, like Eden, soon realized that they were missing.

By the time Lia got to school on Monday, a fine rumor was going around. Lia and Scott had left Fortnightly to make out.

Lia heard it from Missy.

"Make out! That's crazy. We went home and worked on our stamps. Who started this rumor anyway?"

Missy looked uncomfortable. "I heard it from a couple of kids. I don't know who started it."

"It wasn't Eden, was it?"

"No. I mean, she was one of the people who told me, but I don't think she started it."

Lia wondered if that was true.

"I told the other girls you were just friends. . . ." Missy's voice dribbled off as if she wasn't quite sure she believed it herself.

"This is just stupid," Lia fumed. "I'm going to put an end to this."

But how? What was Lia going to do? Take out an ad in the school paper telling everyone they were being silly? She decided there was nothing to do, so whenever she saw kids whispering as she walked by, she just ignored them and pretended they were talking about someone else.

Scott must have heard the rumors too because he didn't look her way all day. After school, though, they met in Lia's backyard. By this time, Lia was mad at Scott. "Oh, we'll just dance out and no one will notice," Lia said bitterly.

Scott was contrite. "I thought it was a good idea. I guess I was wrong."

Lia softened. Scott looked miserable. "So now what do we do?" she asked, her tone less hostile.

"Tell people it's not true?"

Lia gave him a look.

"Yeah. Well, I suppose it will fade in a couple of days. Maybe we should stay away from each other until then."

"I guess." It didn't seem fair, but Lia didn't have any other suggestions.

That was the second thing that Scott was wrong about. For some reason this was a rumor that picked up strength like a hurricane. The next day, Missy told Lia that the kids were saying Lia and Scott had gone into the boys' bathroom to make out.

"You're kidding!" Lia said, appalled. "That's absolutely gross."

"Somebody said they saw you."

The girls were in the library. Their class had gone to pick out books. Missy and Lia were standing in the corner, and Missy was looking around furtively. "I'm not really supposed to be talking to you," Missy said apologetically.

"Why not?"

"Eden said it wasn't a good idea."

"Oh, that's just great," Lia muttered.

"I told her you would never do anything like make out in a bathroom, but Eden said, even if you didn't, everyone thought you did, so we shouldn't be seen with you."

Lia felt tears coming to her eyes. "How can I prove that I didn't do anything?"

"I don't know," Missy said helplessly.

When lunchtime arrived, Lia didn't have the nerve to sit down with the girls. Not when she knew how they believed all the stupid talk going around. She took her tray over to a corner and pretended she was invisible. But she apparently wasn't doing a good enough job. At the end of lunch period, the eighth-grade boy she had danced with at Fortnightly slid into the seat next to her.

"What are you doing here?" she asked, startled.

"Just thought I'd say hello. My name is Max."

There was no point in telling him her name. She was sure he already knew it. "What do you want?"

"I thought maybe you'd like to go to the movies with me sometime."

Lia wanted to wipe that lopsided smile off his face. She knew that he only wanted to take her to the movies so he could see if the rumors were true.

"No thanks," she said, throwing her leftovers into her brown paper bag.

"Why not? We could have fun."

"I don't think so."

Lia picked up her tray and walked away from the boy, wondering if she had done herself any good or if she had just made him mad.

Somehow she got through the rest of the day. As soon as the last bell rang, she was out the door, pretending she had blinders on so she didn't have to look anyone in the eye.

The house was empty when she arrived. Both her parents were still at work. Lia was glumly pouring herself a drink when the phone rang.

"Hey, Lia," Kathy's voice bubbled over the wire. "Trick-or-treat."

"What?"

"Trick-or-treat," Kathy said unsurely. "We are still on for Halloween in Maple Park on Friday, aren't we?"

Oh lord, Lia thought. With everything else that was going on, she had forgotten that this Friday was Halloween. Now what? Maybe she should tell Kathy the whole thing was off. But if she did that, it would be the end of the Holiday Five, and she wouldn't get to see the few friends she did have.

"Yes, we're on."

"Lia, you sound weird. Is something wrong?"

Lia was tempted to confide. But she didn't want to tell the whole horrible story. What if Kathy thought it was true?

"No, everything's fine," Lia said, trying to sound more upbeat.

"I talked to Erin. She said you'll have some costumes there."

"Yes." She explained about the clothes in the attic. "There's plenty of stuff for all of us."

"Okay. Well, I'll just bring my pajamas and toothbrush. I hope Maddy remembers hers."

"Huh?" Then Lia recalled how Maddy had packed her toothbrush on the last day of camp. "Oh, yeah," she said lamely, trying to act as if she had gotten the joke.

She didn't fool Kathy. "Are you sure everything's all right?" Kathy asked with concern.

"Sure," Lia said. "Look, I'm really looking forward to seeing you. All of you. We'll have fun."

When she hung up, she took her cola and went to her room. Outside her window, she caught sight of Scott throwing Skip a Frisbee. She turned away and flopped down on her bed. How had things gotten so screwed up?

There was a moment on Wednesday and on Thursday, after Lia had woken up but before she opened her eyes, that she was happy. But as soon as she had thrown off the covers, all the bad things that had happened in the last couple of days came rushing back to her.

The snickers when she walked by in the hall. The way that the girls pretended she didn't exist. For all she knew, there were even more horrible rumors going around. The worst, though, was Scott's face when she walked by him in the hall, with its mix of pity and embarrassment. No one seemed to be making jokes about him, Lia noticed. It wasn't fair.

The more she thought about that, the angrier she got, especially when she saw one of the boys high-fiving Scott at his locker after school. She didn't know for a fact that their laughter had anything to do with her. It probably didn't. But just seeing Scott in a crowd of friends while the girls treated her like a ghost made Lia so mad, she could feel her head start to ache.

It wasn't easy to make Lia angry, but she was angry now. As soon as she saw Scott walk back into his house, she marched over there and rapped at the door. Finally, he opened it.

"I want to talk to you, Scott," Lia hissed.

"My mother's home," he replied, looking over his shoulder.

"Then come over to my house. No one's home there." Scott followed her across the yard.

She faced him in the living room. "How come everyone's talking about me, and no one thinks *you've* done anything wrong?" she demanded.

Scott shrugged helplessly. "I don't know."

"Has anyone said anything to you?"

"Some of the kids have."

"And what do you tell them?"

Now Scott was all embarrassment. "I say it's not what they think."

Lia was incredulous. "You mean you don't say that it's all a big lie? You haven't told anyone that we didn't do anything in the bathroom?"

"I say we never went in the bathroom. Who would want to make out in the bathroom?"

"What about the rest of it? Scott, we danced out of there to go home and work on our stamps. Do you let people think we really did leave to make out?"

Scott suddenly seemed very interested in the design on the carpet. "I don't say we made out."

"But you don't deny it."

"Well, not exactly."

Lia felt all the anger whoosh out of her like air out of a balloon. She willed him to look up at her, and he finally did. "I thought we were friends," she said quietly.

"Aw, Lia, you don't understand how it is with boys. They would think I was some kind of a wuss if I said nothing happened."

There was a silence that seemed to go on for a long time. Then Lia said, "I guess I don't understand."

"Everybody will forget about it, Lia."

"When?"

"Soon, I guess."

"Soon. I wonder how long that is." Lia sighed. "I think you better go home, Scott."

Scott didn't argue. "Yeah, I told my mom I'd clean up my room."

"Fine." Lia didn't say good-bye. She just stomped upstairs and flung herself on her bed.

Why did things always get worse just when you thought they couldn't get any worse? Out of all the awful things that had happened in the last week, having a fight with Scott was the final straw. They had been friends since they were seven and hardly ever argued. Not about who got to spend more time on Scott's swing set when they were younger, not even when Scott accidentally set his glass of soda down on one of her best stamps and ruined it. She could hardly believe that they were having a fight now.

Lia heard her mother come in, but she didn't get up. Only when she smelled her mother's spaghetti sauce wafting up the stairs did she make any effort to go downstairs. An idea was starting to form.

"Lia, are you all right?" Mrs. Greene asked, seeing her silhouetted against the light from the hall.

"Not too good."

Mrs. Greene came over to Lia and felt her forehead. "You don't feel hot."

"I just feel achy."

"Oh dear. Your friends are supposed to come for the weekend tomorrow. Do you want me to call them and cancel?"

"No . . . I don't think so. Maybe I just need to sleep."

"Why don't you do that, sweetheart. Get into your pajamas. If you're not feeling better by tomorrow, we might have to postpone the visit."

"Mmmm." Lia shut her eyes. She heard her mother quietly close the door behind her.

If she played things right, maybe she could miss school tomorrow. Then she could decide if she really wanted the girls to come. The only thing she knew for sure was that she didn't think she could make it through one more day of school.

Her plan went smoothly. Even though Lia was

ravenous from just having soup for dinner, when her mother asked if she felt well enough to go have a little breakfast and go to school, Lia shook her head no.

"I think I need to sleep some more."

Mrs. Greene took Lia's temperature, and when it was normal, she looked at her daughter oddly. But Lia wasn't one to try and get out of school, so all Mrs. Greene said was, "I guess you should stay home today. You don't have any tests, do you?"

Lia shook her head.

"All right then, sleep."

Though she thought she was all slept out, Lia did catch another short nap. When she awoke, she could feel her stomach rumbling and she knew she couldn't stay in bed one more second. It was time to make her next move.

She threw on a robe and headed downstairs. Her mother was reading the newspaper.

"How are you feeling?" Mrs. Greene asked, taking off her glasses.

"Better, I think. Hungry."

"What do you feel like? Maybe you should have something light like tea and toast?"

"Well, I could start with that." She had the tea and

toast, then asked for an egg, and then popped a cookie into her mouth from the package that was sitting on the table.

"Lia, what's really going on?"

Lia looked up, a few crumbs in the corner of her mouth.

"What do you mean?"

"You may not have been feeling well, but that's not the reason you stayed home."

Lia hated it when her mother did that. Looked right inside her brain and saw all the things that she was trying to keep hidden. Didn't her mother know that it wasn't just that she wanted to keep secrets, although that was part of it? Her mother always seemed so hurt when bad things happened to Lia. When Lia had been sitting home last year, it was almost as if her mother didn't have any friends either. Lia could bear this whole idiotic mix-up about making out with Scott. But she wasn't sure her mother could.

"I needed a mental health day," Lia finally said. "Daddy says that sometimes when he wants to stay home from work and he's not really sick."

"And why did you need a mental health day?" Mrs. Greene asked. "Did something happen at school?"

"Kind of," Lia said evasively.

"You had that sleepover with Eden and Missy. I thought things were getting better. But they haven't called lately. You haven't seen much of Scott either."

Who did her mother think she was, Sherlock Holmes?

"You don't have to tell me if you don't want to. But you might feel better if you did." Her mother sounding so wistful broke through the armor around Lia's heart.

"You promise you won't get upset if I tell you?"

Mrs. Greene crossed her heart. "Promise."

Before she could stop herself, the whole story came pouring out. "It's not fair," Lia finished in a burst. "I didn't do anything."

"I know you didn't."

"And no one's making any rude remarks to Scott. Why's that?" Lia demanded.

"I don't know, Lia. I wish things were different, but for some reason, boys always get off easier than girls when it comes to this sort of thing."

"Well, it's not fair," Lia repeated.

"So what are you going to do about it?" Mrs. Greene asked.

This surprised Lia. She assumed that once she had confided everything, her mother would tell her what to do. "I don't know. I'm trying to ignore the kids who are talking about me and hope they forget about it."

Mrs. Greene nodded approvingly. "I think you're on the right track. Pretty soon there will be something else to talk about."

There was that elusive word *soon* again. "Mom, do you think I should tell the girls not to come for Halloween? I'd hate for them to hear a bunch of stupid rumors about me."

Sipping her coffee, her mother said, "Why don't you just tell them yourself?"

"I couldn't," Lia murmured. "It's too humiliating."

"I'm sure they would support you."

"I don't want them to support me. I just want them to come and have a good time."

Mrs. Greene put down her coffee cup. "It's up to you, Lia. You can do whatever you think is best."

"Jeez, Mom, you don't want me to take a train ride by myself, but now you tell me to figure out all this hard stuff."

Mrs. Greene laughed. "I see what you mean. But

Lia, you have to do what feels right to you. What will you do this weekend if you cancel the visit?"

Lia thought about that for a moment. "Probably stay home and be upset."

"Doesn't sound like much fun."

"No. And I've been looking forward to this since I got home from camp."

Shrugging, Mrs. Greene said, "Well, then . . ."

"Okay, so I won't cancel. But I'm not going to tell them what's going on. I can't. I was popular at camp." Lia could hear her voice starting to shake. "I don't want the girls to know that at home, I'm just a big fat joke."

Her mother reached over and wiped a tear away from Lia's eye. "You know what I think?"

"What?"

"If you're going to have a mental health day, let's really get into it."

Lia was so surprised the tears went away. "Huh?"

Mrs. Greene checked her watch. "I baked some brownies yesterday. Let's have some and watch *All My Children*."

"Mom! I didn't know you watched soaps."

"Oh, sometimes I do. Then let's go out and buy

some groceries for the sleepover. Whatever you think the girls would like. Maybe rent a couple of movies, too. How does that sound?"

It sounded good. Lia felt better than she had in a while. Maybe this weekend wasn't going to be that bad after all.

EIGHT

If this was what mental health days were like, Lia wanted to have them more often. Knowing that everyone else was slaving over their schoolwork while she was picking out her favorite brand of potato chips made the day especially sweet.

It was also the first time since Monday that the words *making out* weren't drumming through her brain. Now they came and went, like a song tune you wish you could forget, but can't, quite.

She was hopeful she could get through the weekend without ever having to mention the whole miserable story. The only time the Holiday Five would see her classmates was tomorrow night, and everyone would be in costume. Probably no one would say a word to Lia's camp friends. What would happen after the weekend was over, Lia would worry about on Monday.

Lia and her mother arrived home with their arms full of groceries, and with only a couple of hours until the Holiday Five arrived. Kathy's housekeeper was driving Kathy and Maddy down. They would arrive about four-thirty, and then they'd go down to the station to get Erin and Jill, who were taking the train. Her mother had been so nice all day that Lia decided she wouldn't even give her the business about Erin taking the train all the way from Chicago.

After she put the groceries on the counter, Mrs. Greene looked around. "Is there anything we've forgotten? Do you think it's clean enough?"

It was always too clean for Lia's taste. "Mom, it's fine. You should see how we lived all summer."

Mrs. Greene gave a small shudder. "I prefer not to think about it, thanks."

"I wonder what the other girls' houses look like," Lia said, as she began to put things into the refrigerator.

"Well, Kathy's, I imagine, is pretty nice."

"She once said something about tennis courts. And she's got a housekeeper."

"What does her father do?" Mrs. Greene asked as she got out a bowl to make her peanut butter brownies.

Lia shrugged. "I don't know. Her parents are divorced. She and her mom live in Lake Pointe and her dad lives in the city with his wife and their children."

"That must be hard on her," Mrs. Greene said sympathetically.

"She doesn't talk too much about it."

"Tell me about the other girls, while we bake," Mrs. Greene said.

As Lia helped get out the ingredients, she told her mother about Maddy's weight problem, and how Erin was one of six kids. Some of the things, Mrs. Greene remembered from Lia's letters, but Lia realized there was a lot she hadn't told her mother, like the fact that Maddy's father was dead. The one person she steered clear of talking about was Jill.

Even with all that was going on, Owen's comment about white people still popped into her brain once in a while. Of all the Holiday Five it seemed odd that she would be most nervous about seeing Jill, the one she felt closest to, but she was. Should she tell Jill she had overheard Owen's remark or should she just let it slide? Even if she did want to talk about it, what in the world would she say?

"You haven't said much about Jill," Mrs. Greene commented as she shoved the brownies into the oven.

There was that mother radar again. "Well, you've met Jill."

"I liked her."

"Me too." Lia looked at the clock. "It's almost time for Kathy and Maddy to get here," she said, excitement coloring her voice. "I want to change."

"Well, go ahead."

Lia raced upstairs. She glanced into the guest room. There were twin beds in there. And there were sleeping bags in the attic if the girls all wanted to sleep together. Lia had barely put on her new sweatshirt when her mother called from downstairs, "Lia, Maddy and Kathy are here."

There was a big, huggy reunion in the living room.

"I'm so glad to see you!" Lia squealed.

"Me too," Kathy said, her eyes bright.

"Me three," Maddy added.

Mrs. Greene glanced at her watch. "You have time for a cup of hot chocolate before we go meet the train."

"I'd love some," Maddy said promptly.

The girls sat around the kitchen table and caught up on their news. At least, Kathy and Maddy told what they had been doing. Lia hoped that no one noticed she wasn't saying much. When they were finished with their hot chocolate, they piled into the car to go down to the train station, and arrived just as the train was pulling in.

Erin and Jill were the first ones off the train. There was more hugging and kissing.

Once they got back home, Lia took them on a tour of the house.

"I love Victorian houses," Maddy said, as they came back into the living room. "And all these great antiques."

Mrs. Greene came into the living room. "We've tried to keep the furnishings in the style of the house."

"Is the house very old?" Erin asked.

"Turn of the century. It's filled with stories."

"Like what?" Jill wanted to know.

"I'll let Mr. Greene tell you at dinner," Mrs. Greene said with a smile. "He's the storyteller."

"Oh, not Hansen's ghost," Lia groaned.

"What ghost?" Erin demanded.

Lia shook her head. "The story's too stupid. You're not going to hear it from me."

"Have the girls unpacked?" Mrs. Greene asked Lia.

"Not exactly." The girls had thrown their stuff in a big heap in the corner of her room.

"Well, why don't you take care of that, and by then your father will be home and we'll be ready for dinner."

"What are the sleeping arrangements?" Jill asked as the girls got their bags in Lia's room.

"Where should we put our things?" Maddy wanted to know.

"I've got sleeping bags if we all want to sleep together, but otherwise, there's the guest room and the foldout bed in my father's den."

Maddy, Kathy, and Erin put their things in the guest room, but Jill stayed with Lia in her room.

"You can unpack in here," Lia told her.

"I didn't know what to bring," Jill said, as she pulled a couple of things out of her suitcase. "Sometimes it seems like all I've got is skating things."

Since Jill brought it up, Lia said, "I didn't really get a chance to tell you at the rink how great your skating was."

"Yeah, you did," Jill said, pulling on a clean sweatshirt. "I think I'll put this on for dinner."

But Lia didn't want to get off the subject of that

Saturday quite so quickly. Lia wasn't sure why she wanted to press it; she felt nervous just thinking about bringing up Owen's comment. But she had to find out just a little more about what went on that afternoon, if she could do it without being too obvious. She could see now it would bother her all weekend if she didn't. "Did your brother like the exhibition?" Lia asked.

Jill shrugged. "He's proud of me, but he's a typical big brother. Always trying to push me around. 'Do this, sister, do that, sister,' " she quoted mockingly.

"So you're not very close."

Jill looked surprised at that. "No, we are. Owen can be a pain, but we stick together like honey. Always have."

"Oh." Lia turned away and pretended to fuss with her hair, but really, she didn't want Jill to see how disappointed she was. She had been hoping that Jill would say Owen was just a brother with a big mouth, someone whose opinion didn't count very much. Apparently, though, his opinion did count.

Erin stuck her head in the door. "Ready?"

"Sure," Lia said, relieved, now, that her conversation with Jill was going to be cut off.

The dining-room table was set with her mother's

best china and the last of the mums were in a vase on the table. Lia was proud that everything looked so nice. She could smell the delicious aroma of her mother's spaghetti sauce coming from the kitchen.

"Gee, this is so pretty," Erin said quietly.

Lia glanced at Erin, who was usually so confident. Surely a few mums and a lace tablecloth weren't intimidating her, were they?

Mrs. Greene came out of the kitchen. "Why don't you take a seat? Lia's father just got home."

As if on cue, Mr. Greene came downstairs. Lia introduced him all around. When they sat down at the table, Maddy said a bit shyly, "Mrs. Greene said you'd tell us about the ghost in the house."

"Oh, Hansen's ghost," Mr. Greene said, taking some salad from the bowl that was being passed around. "That's an interesting story."

"Dad—" Lia began. She thought the story was dumb.

Jill cut her off. "No, we want to hear it."

"Of course we do," Kathy added.

"Oh, go ahead and tell them," Lia grumbled. "They'll never forget about it now."

Mr. Greene settled back in his chair. "This house had been in the family of the people we bought it from more than one hundred years. They were retiring, but he didn't want the stories about it to be lost, so he told me some of them."

"I think he made them up," Lia muttered.

Ignoring her, Mr. Greene continued. "The house was built by the man's grandfather before the turn of the century. His name was Hansen. He built this house for his bride, Justine. But Justine wasn't happy here. She had come from New York, and she was lost and lonely, and always longing to go back home. After she had two children, she decided she just couldn't stay in the house anymore, and went home to New York to visit her family. She planned to stay, but Mr. Hansen loved her so much, he went to New York and begged her to come back."

"This is so romantic," Maddy sighed.

"It has a bad end," Lia informed her friends.

"She came," Mr. Greene went on. "Unwillingly, but she came. One day, she went up to the attic. No one knows why. But when they found her, later that day, she had fallen out of the window. Or jumped. Ever since, people who've lived in this house say they've seen a woman with long, blonde hair, dressed in a white nightgown, floating around the attic, murmuring about home."

There was a moment of silence after Mr. Greene finished.

"That was better than the ghost stories we heard at camp," Erin whispered.

"And it's true," Mrs. Greene said. Although usually the no-nonsense type, Mrs. Greene had a definite superstitious streak.

"Mom, how can you say that? You've never seen her." Lia turned to the girls. "My Uncle Danny calls this story 'The Case of the Headless Hansen.' "

"She had her head," Mrs. Greene said indignantly. "Besides, how do you know I haven't seen her?"

"Have you?" Jill asked.

"Well, no, but I think it makes an appropriate story for Halloween, don't you?"

Kathy turned to Mr. Greene. "Do you think the ghost is real?"

"There are more things in heaven and earth . . ." he said, quoting *Hamlet*.

Maddy sighed. "Gee, a real live ghost."

The others broke out in laughter.

"It's not live," Lia finally said, "and I don't believe it's real."

Erin disagreed. "I believe in ghosts. I'm Irish. I believe in leprechauns and banshees."

"I don't know about banshees, but I want to find more about this ghost," Jill said. "Let's check out the attic."

Kathy looked a little nervous. "I don't know. What if—"

"We have to go up after dinner and look for costumes, anyway. Then you'll see there isn't any ghost," Lia said, stabbing at a meatball with her fork. "It's just a plain old attic."

After the girls had stuffed themselves at dinner, they went upstairs. The attic was large, running the length of the whole house. Mrs. Greene tried to keep it neat, but it was crammed with furniture, old suitcases, and cardboard boxes.

"Which window was it?" Maddy demanded.

Lia sighed. "Oh, Maddy."

"I want to know, too," Erin chimed in.

"All right, all right." Lia marched over to a long, narrow window that overlooked a rose garden at the back of the house. "It was this window."

Jill peered out and gave a little shiver. "It's sure a long way down."

"This window is so narrow," Maddy noted. "Mrs. Hansen must have been awfully thin."

Kathy moved next to Jill. "How would anyone have the nerve to jump out of a window?"

"Maybe she was pushed," Erin said happily.

"Erin!" Lia exclaimed.

"I know, Lia, but it makes a better story."

"She wasn't pushed; she probably didn't even jump. I think she just tripped or something and fell out," Lia said.

Jill looked at her doubtfully. "That doesn't seem possible."

"Do you guys want to keep talking about Mrs. Hansen or do you want to find some Halloween costumes?" Lia asked, trying to change the subject. She hated the thought of some ghost running around her house.

Erin and Jill exchanged looks. It was clear which they wanted to do, but neither of them had the nerve to say so. Kathy finally broke the silence and said, "Let's see some of these great clothes."

"Fine," Lia said with relief.

In a few minutes they had pulled out some boxes and were rummaging through them.

"Oh, here's something from the roaring twenties," Erin called. She pulled out a sleeveless black dress covered with a fringe that shimmered and swayed as she shook it out.

"Cool!" Maddy exclaimed. "Can I try it on?"

"I found it," Erin said.

"It's too big for you," Maddy pointed out.

"Well, it's too small for you," Erin rejoined.

Lia knew that sometimes Erin's tongue moved faster than her brain, and this was one of them. Maddy looked hurt.

"I think it's my size," Lia said, trying to diffuse the situation.

"Put it on." Kathy quickly jumped in.

Lia tossed off her sweatshirt and jeans. She wasn't embarrassed. The girls had dressed and undressed together all summer. Slipping the dress over her head, she wriggled into it. It fit perfectly.

"Terrific," Jill said.

Lia looked around at the other girls.

Erin was nodding. "It wouldn't look any better on me."

Kathy fished around in the trunk. "Look at this." She handed Lia a feathered headband. "I guess they wore these with the dresses when they were doing the Charleston."

"I love it!" Lia quickly put it on. "There's a mirror up over there. I want to see." She ran over to it and twirled around. "This one's mine, okay?"

"Well, now that you're fixed up, what about the rest of us?" Jill demanded.

"There's boxes of stuff. Go to it."

The next hour was an orgy of trying on, flinging off, oohing and aahing. By the time they were finished, the Holiday Five were exhausted, but they all had costumes to wear.

Kathy had found a white Victorian blouse with muttonchop sleeves, which she matched with a long, black taffeta skirt. The blouse had belonged to Lia's great-grandmother.

"My mother has a brooch and earrings I'll bet she'll let you wear with this," Lia said. "It'll be perfect."

"We can put your hair up in some kind of an old-fashioned do," Jill said.

Jill had found Lia's grandmother's navy uniform from World War II. She looked adorable in it.

Maddy had some problems finding a costume. Nothing really fit her properly, and for a while, Lia was worried that there would be nothing for her to wear. But by putting together some odds and ends, a silk scarf to wear around her head, an off-the-shoulder white blouse, a long patchwork skirt, and lots of beads, she transformed herself into a gypsy.

"Are you sure my costume is all right?" Erin said, squinting into the tarnished mirror.

"You look great," Lia assured her.

Erin stared back at her reflection. Wearing a man's white shirt, a vest, wool knickers and a beat-up cap, Erin was going to the Halloween shindig as a newsboy.

"But will people know what I'm supposed to be?" Erin asked doubtfully.

"They will when you have a pile of newspapers under your arm." Kathy said.

"Just go around yelling, 'Extra, extra, read all about it,' " Maddy suggested.

"I'm sure Lia's friends will like that," Erin said with a giggle. "We don't want them to think she went to camp with a bunch of nerds."

The other girls laughed along with her, but Lia didn't. All the sick feelings of the last week came rushing back at her. Not only didn't she have any friends to speak of, she was the most notorious girl in the seventh grade. Kids at the community center might be laughing, but it wouldn't be at Erin yelling "extra." It would be at Lia for having the nerve to show up at all.

No one seemed to notice her change of mood. They continued to chatter on about their costumes. Finally, it seemed as a good hostess Lia should move the party downstairs. "So what do you want to do now?" she asked, trying to sound upbeat. "I rented some movies for us."

"I'm getting kind of tired," Kathy answered.

"Don't be such a party pooper," Erin scoffed.

"It's too early to go to bed," Maddy agreed.

Erin clapped her hands together. "Hey, I have a great idea. Let's watch the movie till we get really tired, then, instead of sleeping in our rooms, let's bring the sleeping bags up and sleep in the attic."

"Oh let's," Maddy said enthusiastically.

"You want to see the ghost," Lia groaned.

"Who knows when we'll ever have another chance?" Jill said.

"Let me get this straight. We've got perfectly good beds downstairs, but instead you want to sleep in this stuffy attic, on the hard floor, on the off chance, and I do mean off, that we might see a ghost. Is that right?" Lia asked.

"That's it," Erin said brightly.

"It's almost Halloween," Maddy added. "If a ghost is ever going to show up, it would be tonight."

Lia turned to Kathy. She hadn't seemed all that excited about ghosts at dinner.

"It would be kind of cool," Kathy said with a shrug.

Lia sighed. "I guess I can't be a bad hostess and say no, but I swear, if I can't sleep, I'm going right to my bed."

"Then you'll miss all the excitement," Erin warned.

"I'll miss breaking my back," Lia answered, but she added, "If my parents say it's okay, we'll do it."

Erin and Maddy scrambled downstairs, with Kathy right behind them. Jill walked beside Lia, who was taking her time.

"Is something wrong?" Jill asked.

"What do you mean?" Lia asked evasively.

"I don't know. Just not your good old self, I guess."

Jill looked so concerned, so ready to listen that Lia admitted, "Some things have been going on."

"Like what?"

But before Lia could answer, Erin came up to them. Lia felt relieved at the interruption. "We asked your mom about sleeping up here. She said it was okay."

"She asked if she could join us," Maddy added.

"You're kidding," Lia said, appalled.

"Well, she was, I think," Kathy said, joining them. "But I bet she would have liked to."

They started to watch the movie, but halfway through, Maddy started yawning.

"We'd better get upstairs," Erin urged, "before we fall asleep."

"Yeah, we can watch the rest of the movie tomorrow," Jill agreed.

So half an hour later, Lia and the rest of the Holiday Five were trying to get comfortable on the wooden floor of the attic. Erin had even insisted that Lia open the window, so the ghost could get in, even though Lia had pointed out that a ghost could walk through walls if it wanted to. Lia opened the window anyway. It was hot in the attic.

"Shall we shut off the lights?" Jill asked.

"Of course we should," Erin insisted. "The ghost might not come if there's a light on."

Lia rolled her eyes, but she got up and turned off the lights.

"Let's talk until we're sleepy," Jill suggested, punching her pillow.

Lia knew this would be a perfect time to confide, but the girls were being so silly and having so much fun, she couldn't bear to change the mood. They started talking about what they had been up to lately, but soon the conversation slowed to murmurs. Lia could feel her eyes closing. The heavy, hot air was putting her, and the others, to sleep.

Just as Lia was drifting off, she felt someone grab at her arm. Sitting bolt upright, she said, "What?"

Maddy said in a quavery voice, "I saw it. The ghost."

"Oh you're just imagining things."

"No. I saw a white gauzy thing float by."

"It's too dark to see anything."

"But I heard something, too, kind of a crying noise."

By now, Jill was up, Kathy and Erin too.

"I saw Justine," Maddy hissed.

"Are you sure?" Erin whispered.

"Where?" Jill demanded.

"Right there!"

To Lia's amazement, in the darkest corner of the room, a filmy piece of white material was jerking back and forth. The sound of a small cry rose through the air from the same corner.

"It's her!" Maddy shrieked.

The girls were clutching each other.

"Maybe it's just the wind," Kathy said, her voice quavering.

"Then what's that noise?" Jill demanded.

The high-pitched whimper came once more.

"Wait a minute," Lia said, sitting up a little straighter. "I know that noise." She got up and moved toward the corner.

"Don't!" Maddy said, clutching Lia's leg.

Lia shook herself free and ran toward the wafting shape. She pulled at it while the other girls watched, terrified.

"That's what I thought." Lia reached down and freed something from the material. Flower sprang free and raced down the attic stairs.

"Oh lord," Jill said, falling back on her pillow.

The girls started laughing and couldn't stop. It was less from amusement than relief.

"I don't think I want to stay up here anymore," Kathy finally said, when she caught her breath.

"Me either," Erin agreed.

"Well, I never wanted to sleep up here at all," Lia reminded them. "Can we just go downstairs now?"

Silently, the girls gathered their things. They decided they all wanted to put their sleeping bags in Lia's room. They weren't quite over the "ghost" yet.

"I hope I don't have any bad dreams," Maddy said.

"If you do, I'll give you a major poke," Erin told her. "Let's go to sleep."

Lia was so tired, she barely had time to whisper good night to Jill before she dozed off. The next thing she knew, the sun was streaming in the window and Jill was shaking her. "Wake up, sleepy."

Lia opened her eyes. "Good morning, Dopey."

Jill giggled. "Now we just have to wake Grouchy, Happy, and Sneezy, and we can get this day going." Jill looked at her expectantly, but Lia just wanted to roll over. The last thing she wanted was for this day to begin.

NINE

"So what do you want to do today, girls?" Mrs. Greene asked at breakfast. Mr. Greene had prepared his Saturday special, waffles covered with bananas and gobs of butter and syrup. The girls were digging in.

"I want to see Maple Park," Erin said.

"I thought we could walk downtown," Lia said slowly. She hoped they wouldn't run into anyone she knew.

"That sounds like a good idea," Kathy said. "We should walk off these waffles."

"As if you needed to," Maddy said enviously. "I don't know how you stay so thin."

Kathy shrugged. "It's in the genes."

"With me it's in the jeans," Maddy sighed, patting her behind.

As the girls were getting their jackets out of the closet, Erin said, glancing out the window, "Ooh. Who's that cute boy?"

Lia didn't even have to look. "That's Scott. He lives next door."

"Your friend, right?" Jill asked. "The one who sent you all those postcards."

"Why didn't you tell us he was so adorable?" Kathy demanded.

"He wasn't. At least when I left for camp, he wasn't. He had a metamorphosis over the summer." Lia was studying insects in science.

"Well, let's go meet him," Erin said, opening the door.

"I don't think we should," Lia said nervously.

Four pair of eyes turned in her direction. "Why not?" Maddy asked.

That was stupid, Lia thought. Of course, they'd want to meet Scott.

"Oh, we might all scare him. In a group, I mean," she added lamely.

The girls were still looking at her, puzzled.

"I'm being silly. Let's go."

Scott was sitting on his steps, playing a video game. Actually, Lia hadn't been that far off base. Scott did look a little nervous when he saw the girls coming toward him.

Lia hoped Scott wasn't going to embarrass her. "I told you my friends were coming," she said stiffly. "This is Kathy, Erin, Jill, and Maddy."

"Hello," Scott murmured.

"What are you playing?" Erin asked in a friendly fashion.

Scott handed over his game. "It's called Combat. It's new."

While Erin was playing with the game, Kathy asked politely, "Are you going to the community center tonight?"

"I'm not sure yet," he replied cautiously.

"Well, you should come," Maddy said. "Lia has been telling us how much fun it's going to be."

"She has?" Scott asked, surprised.

Jill frowned. "Why, don't you think it's going to be fun?"

"Oh, sure. It'll be great."

"Then why aren't you coming?" Erin said, handing the game back.

"I . . . I might have something else to do."

Even Erin wasn't bold enough to ask what.

"Maybe I'll see you there," Scott finally said.

The girls said good-bye. When they were out of earshot, Maddy said, "I guess I see why you didn't want to introduce us."

"You do?" Lia asked with surprise.

"Sure. He's so shy."

"Something like that," Lia murmured under her breath.

As the girls walked downtown, they saw lots of little trick-or-treaters out in all their Halloween finery.

"Ooh, look at them," Maddy cooed.

Three little bunnies, the youngest being carried by her mother, were coming toward them, eager, excited expressions on their whiskered faces.

"They're so cute," Erin said. "What was your favorite costume when you were young?"

"I loved being a witch," Maddy replied. "My mother made the costume, but the best part was this long black wig she found for me to wear. I thought it was so neat having that fake hair flying all around."

Maddy turned toward Kathy. "What about you?"

Kathy answered promptly. "A princess."

"That figures," Erin laughed.

Kathy ignored her. "I had this gorgeous pink dress with little stars sewn on it."

"No wig for you, I bet," Jill guessed.

"Nope. My mother curled my hair in these big, fat sausage curls. They looked great with a crown."

"I had an outfit my grandmother brought me from Switzerland," Lia remembered. "It was all hand embroidered. I always felt like Heidi when I wore it."

"My best costume was a television," Maddy said.

The girls looked at her.

"You were a television?" Erin queried.

Maddy nodded happily. "My grandfather made it out of a big cardboard box. And my mother draped brown material around my legs, so it looked like the TV was on a pedestal. I had an antenna, knobs, everything."

"What was on you?" Lia asked. "I mean on your screen?"

"Oh, that was the best. My grandfather cut out full-page pictures from magazines, and he put them on kind of a roller. When someone twisted my knob, the picture changed."

"Wow," Erin said, impressed. "I never had a best costume. I always got the hand-me-downs my sister wore the year before."

"What about you, Jill?" Kathy asked. "What was your favorite costume?"

"A clown, I guess," she replied with a shrug.

It was plain that the clown costume hadn't been that much of a favorite costume. The look on Jill's face wasn't exactly saying happy memories. For a few seconds Lia's mind was off herself and she was wondering why Jill looked so down.

"Well, here we are," Lia said, glad to get off a subject that was so obviously unpleasant for Jill. "This is it, downtown Maple Park."

"It's cute," Maddy said.

Lia looked around. It was kind of cute, with its quaint brick buildings that housed antiques shops, specialty stores and little cafés. She guessed she had lived here so long, she didn't really notice.

But the girls had a great time ducking into the shops and picking out things they'd like to buy. They especially liked a store called Kitty. All the merchandise, the pins, the earrings, the pillows, books, even the clothes featured cats.

"I love these earrings," Kathy squealed. "They look just like my cat, Carolyn. I'm going to get them."

Lia caught sight of Erin's expression as Kathy paid for the earrings. They weren't cheap. Lia knew that

Erin would probably have had to save for ages to pay for a pair of earrings like that.

After looking through almost every store in Maple Park, Maddy said, "Are we going to have lunch?"

"I'm still full from breakfast," Kathy said, "but I guess I could eat something."

Lia took them to a small restaurant that featured soups and sandwiches. They were the youngest patrons by about twenty years. Lia had picked it deliberately. Most of the kids hung out at the hot dog stand down the street. Lia felt sure that she was safe from the kids at school in this establishment. After lunch, they decided to go to a movie. It was a cheapie theater that only cost two dollars, but it was featuring a comedy that none of them had seen. After the movie, they lounged around for a while, and then it was time to get ready for the Halloween festivities.

Now that the time to actually go to the community center had arrived, Lia could feel all her fear hitting her like a bullet. Why had she let this happen? she wondered. Why hadn't she just cancelled the whole stupid thing?

No one seemed to notice how nervous Lia was. Giggling and putting on plenty of makeup, the girls were all excited about getting into their costumes.

Maddy showed surprising skill at putting Kathy's hair up in a fancy twist that looked old-fashioned, yet pretty at the same time. After admiring her hairdo in a hand mirror, Kathy said to Lia, "How do you want your hair? Maybe Maddy could put yours up too. That would look nice with the head piece."

"I don't know if I'm going tonight," Lia heard herself say.

"What!" Jill exclaimed.

"I'm getting a really bad headache," Lia said.

"So take some aspirin," Maddy suggested. "I've got some in my purse."

Lia shook her head. "I get these sometimes. Aspirin doesn't really help."

A gypsy, newsboy, Victorian lady and World War II Wave looked at Lia with disappointment.

"Well, we're not going if you don't," Kathy said.

"No, no," Lia protested. "Don't stay home because of me. My mom will drive you."

"Lia, don't be silly," Jill said. "It wouldn't be any fun without you."

"We're not going to just leave you here," Kathy added.

"Of course not," Jill said. "We'll just stay home, maybe play cards or something if you feel up to it."

As much as Lia wanted to say, "Great! Cut the deck," she knew she couldn't. What was she thinking of? Here were her friends, all dressed up, looking forward to some Halloween excitement, excitement promised by Lia Denise Greene, and she was ready to keep them home, playing Hearts.

Looking at her friends, all so concerned, Lia wished she had just told the girls the truth, but it was too late for that now. Her mother was calling upstairs saying, "Girls, get a move on or you're going to be late."

Lia made a determined effort to smile. "Maddy is right. Maybe all I need is some aspirin."

"Are you sure?" Kathy asked with concern. "We don't want you to go and be miserable."

"No, I'm sure I'll be fine," Lia said. "I'll go get the aspirin." She went to the bathroom and took some. Actually, she did have the beginnings of a headache.

Mrs. Greene drove them over to the community center. "You all look so great!" she exclaimed when she saw them trooping down the stairs. She ran and got her camera so she could take pictures. "I should open a vintage clothing store in the attic."

"Just make sure Flower stays out of the attic," Lia told her mother.

"No, no," Erin corrected. "Let Flower come up

whenever she wants to. Then you can charge extra if any of the customers see the ghost."

"What time do you want to be picked up?" Mrs. Greene asked as she pulled into a parking space.

How about an hour, Lia said to herself. "I'll call."

"All right. Have a good time."

"We will," the girls chorused as they entered the brightly lit community center.

"Well, it sure looks like you've got a good turn-out tonight," Erin said, as she watched the kids streaming into the gym.

If the rest of the community center was well lit, the gym was spooky and dark. All the lights had been dimmed, and someone had done a terrific job of decorating the gym with ghosts and witches hanging from the ceiling, and giant carved jack-o'-lanterns standing guard at festively papered tables heaping with food.

The DJ had already started playing records, and unlike the kids at the Fortnightly, no one was waiting around to dance. The floor was already full.

"Do you see any of your friends?" Kathy asked, looking around.

Lia did. There was Eden, in what she obviously must have felt was a bit of typecasting, wearing a queen's outfit, complete with crown and robe. Several of the girls from her class were with her.

"Uh . . ." Lia answered, beginning to perspire a little. How long did she think she could keep this up?

Just then Missy walked by dressed as a hobo. Missy probably wouldn't say anything horrible. She could introduce her. "Oh, Missy."

Missy turned to look at her. "Hi, Lia."

"Missy, these are my friends from camp." She introduced them all around.

"Pretty cool party," Jill said.

"Yeah," Missy replied, looking in Eden's direction. Obviously, she felt as if she shouldn't be seen with this particular group.

The DJ interrupted them. "Time for games, everyone. The first one is bobbing for apples. Anyone who wants to bob, get in line. Everyone else, come on and watch."

It was mostly boys who enjoyed getting wet doing the bobbing, but the rest of the kids gathered around, cheering on their favorites. Then it was time for a giant game of musical chairs. Lia thought musical chairs might be a little babyish, but she had never played it before to rock music, nor with so many people, and certainly not with them in costume. It wasn't every day you got to see a Coke bottle trying to push Madonna off a chair. In another mood, she would have enjoyed it. At least all the hubbub made it impossible to notice no one was talking to her.

The musical chairs game ended with Erin and a boy tying for first place. She walked off with a giant bag of candy corn as a prize.

"That was great," Erin said, her eyes shining. "And it made me hungry. Let's go over and grab some food."

The tables were crowded, but the girls pushed their way in and got some sandwiches and chips. Maddy jostled against Scott. He wasn't wearing a costume, unless you counted the baseball cap he was wearing. "Oh, you came after all," she said.

"Yeah. Hi."

"Why don't you sit with us?" Kathy asked. "Jill grabbed a table for us." She indicated the tables that had been set up around the room.

Scott looked over at Lia. She didn't want to sit with him, but it would probably look weird if he declined Kathy's invitation. She gave a small shrug.

"Come on. We haven't really had a chance to talk to any of Lia's friends," Erin said. She turned to Lia. "Maybe we could get some of the other kids to join us."

"There's only six chairs at each table," Lia pointed out. "Just enough for the Holiday Five plus one."

"Oh yeah," Erin said, a little disappointedly. The girls and Scott walked over to the table Jill was saving and put down the food in front of her. "Look who we found," Maddy said.

Just as Lia was about to sit down, a boy dressed as Robin Hood came up to her. She didn't know him. He probably went to the other elementary school in town. Or maybe he was a guest like her friends were.

"Would you like to dance?" he asked.

"No, that's okay. Thanks." She turned to sit down.

"Oh, go ahead," Kathy said.

Lia was about to say, "I don't want to," but the boy looked so uncomfortable, it seemed rude to just give him the brush-off like that.

"All right."

As Robin Hood pushed her back and forth, Lia glanced over at her table. Everyone seemed to be talking and having a good time.

She hadn't said a word to the boy she was dancing with, and she began to feel uncomfortable. Of course, he hadn't said anything to her, either. Still, she felt she had some responsibility to make the next few minutes as pleasant as possible.

"Are you from Maple Park or are you visiting some-one?"

"Visiting."

Lia waited for more. There wasn't any.

"Who?"

"My cousin."

Since he looked like he had no intention of di-vulging the name, Lia desperately cast about in her mind for another avenue of conversation. "You're Robin Hood, right?"

"Right."

"Have you ever read the book?"

The boy looked at her oddly. "He's in a book?"

"Of course. *The Adventures of Robin Hood.*"

"Oh. I thought he was just in a movie." Then he lapsed back into silence.

Lia gave up. There was nothing wrong with a few moments of quiet dancing, she decided.

When the dance was over, Lia headed back to her table. She was horrified by what she saw. There was Max with a couple of his eighth-grade friends, talking to Scott and the girls. She felt like running in the op-posite direction, but Kathy had already spotted her. She willed herself to go over. She didn't have much of a choice.

Max turned to her. "We were just going to ask your friends to dance," he said.

Lia wanted to yell, "Get lost," but she could barely breathe, much less talk.

"Are you as much fun as your friend?" a tall boy named Jed asked Erin with a laugh.

"I guess so," Erin said innocently.

"Wild," Jed grinned. He held out his hand. "Let's go."

But Kathy sensed something wasn't quite right. "What do you mean *fun*?"

"You know, fun. Like her," Max said, gesturing toward Lia. "The hottest girl in Maple Park."

TEN

Jill burst out laughing. "Lia? Hot?" She turned to Lia, trying to swallow her giggles. "Sorry, Lia, but he's kidding, right?"

Lia didn't know what to say, but Max did. "Hey," he said, offended, "I'm not making this up. She and her boyfriend over there"—Max jerked his thumb toward Scott—"they left Fortnightly to make out in the boys' bathroom."

Finally, Lia found her voice, and it was loud. "I did not."

Jeff looked at Scott.

"She did not," Scott's voice was less steady, but quieter.

"What do you mean?" Jeff said with a frown. "My

brother's in your class. He said you didn't deny it."

Scott didn't look at anyone. "I'm denying it now."

Max smiled his crooked smile. "I get it. You made it up. What's the matter? Can't you even get your girl to give you one little, bitty kiss?"

"I'm not his girl!"

"Haven't you ever heard of people being just friends?" Scott added.

The exchange was beginning to draw a crowd. Eden, Missy and a few of the other seventh-grade girls and boys began to wander over.

Lia felt as mad at Max and his idiot friends as she had been that day at Scott. This getting angry stuff was becoming easier. "I think you started these stupid rumors, Max. Maybe you got mad because I didn't like it when you stepped all over me with your big, fat feet!"

Maybe letting loose was easier, but these words were still a surprise. Lia felt her face go all hot and then cold. Max looked as if he couldn't believe what she had said either.

"I think it was the other way around," he snarled. "And hey, I admit it, I was wrong about the rumors. Who'd want to make out with a drip like you!" He stomped off, his friends behind him.

For what seemed like the longest time, no one said anything. Then Erin whispered, "Boy, you Maple Park kids sure know how to throw a party."

That broke the ice. Everyone started talking at once. Jill and Kathy wanted to know the whole story, Lia turned to Scott to thank him for sticking up for her, and Eden said to Missy and the other girls, "I can't believe how rude that Max was. I never really believed all those rumors anyway."

The jabber was interrupted by a blast of music and the DJ inviting everyone back on the dance floor.

"Not me," Lia said fervently. "I'm never going to dance again." Some of the kids started laughing, but this time it was with her, not at her.

"I hope you will," Scott said, under the laughter.

She could tell he was trying to apologize. "I changed my mind. Let's dance."

"Now?" he asked, startled.

"It'll never be safer. Not after that scene."

They moved out on the dance floor. They went so long without saying anything, Lia felt like she was dancing with that Robin Hood guy again.

Finally, Scott said, "After you came over the other day, I thought you'd never talk to me again."

"Me either."

"But now everything's okay?" he asked.

Lia nodded.

They continued to dance, but now the silence was companionable, and they only butted heads once.

When she wasn't looking down at her feet, Lia was looking around the gym. Kathy and Erin were dancing. Jill and Maddy were sitting at the table, talking to Missy. Lia wondered where Eden was.

The rest of the evening passed uneventfully. More games, more dances—though Lia was happy to sit the rest of them out—and prizes for the best costumes. Whenever one of the girls tried to ask her more about The Scene, as Lia was beginning to call it in her mind, she just said, "Later."

Later came when the girls had finally arrived home, taken off their costumes and makeup and gathered in Lia's bedroom. Lia noticed that they had been careful to say nothing in the car as Mr. Greene drove them home, nor when they arrived at the Greenes', and Lia's mother kept bustling in and out, asking questions about the party, and offering them cold cream and mascara remover.

Now, though, they were bursting with questions. They had put out the sleeping bags, though only Maddy had crawled into hers. The other girls were sitting in a circle, surrounding a big plate of Mrs. Greene's peanut butter brownies.

"So, fire away," Lia said.

"Why didn't you tell us?" Erin demanded.

"I couldn't. It was so gross." Then Lia explained what had happened from beginning to end.

"It sounds horrible," Maddy said sympathetically.

"It was," Lia agreed.

Jill pretended to be looking at her nails. "I'm sure it was. But I've got to tell you Lia, I'm a little mad at you."

"Mad?" Erin looked at her. "How can you be mad? Lia's the one that's had the week from hell."

"I know what Jill means," Kathy said soberly.

"Uh-oh," Maddy said. "I think we need to have a bull session, like we did at camp."

Bull sessions were where the girls sat around and talked about whatever was on their minds. Sometimes some surprising things came out of them.

"I think that's a good idea," Erin declared.

Lia didn't like where this was headed. Just when she thought the time for being upset was over. What did they have to be mad about, anyway?

"Well, I don't think it's such a great idea," Lia said grumpily. "But if you insist, then I'm going to go first."

At camp, the person with the most grievances always got to talk first.

Kathy said, "All right."

"You saw what I went through tonight," Lia scolded. "Are you going to make it worse now?"

Kathy turned to her. "One reason tonight was so bad was because you didn't tell us what was going on. We could have helped you."

"I told you, I was embarrassed," Lia argued.

"I can understand that," Maddy said quietly. "When you're embarrassed about something, you just hope it goes away."

Erin said, "Like if you have a pimple. You don't, like, draw a big circle around it."

"I don't think telling something to your friends is the same thing," Kathy told her.

"They're not really your friends unless you're honest with them," Jill added.

"Do you really think that?" Lia wanted to know.

"Of course."

"Then I've got something I want you to tell the truth about." Lia got out the words before she could change her mind.

"What?" Jill asked curiously.

Lia was finally going to get her chance to find out

about Owen's remark. This was a bull session, where you were supposed to say whatever was on your mind. None of the other girls was holding back. Why should she?

"That day I saw you skate, after the exhibition was over, I came back inside the rink to ask you how to get to the library."

"I didn't see you," Jill said.

"I saw you first. And I heard your brother say something about hanging around with white people. It didn't sound like he liked white people very much."

All eyes turned in Jill's direction. She was clearly surprised. "Yeah, I'm not going to deny it. Owen's like that," she said with a sigh.

"So how do you feel about being friends with us?" Lia asked.

Jill spoke carefully. "I'll be straight with you. It's not always easy. I told you that, Lia. But I pick my friends by who I like, and I don't care what anybody says, not even Owen."

"Why doesn't your brother like white people?" Maddy asked curiously.

"My brother's had a lot of stuff happen to him. People making nasty remarks. Sometimes worse. But he's never really had any white friends like I have to balance things out. He just doesn't think whites and blacks should hang out together."

"I'm glad you don't feel that way," Maddy said.

Jill clasped her hands together. "Remember this afternoon when we were talking about our favorite costumes? I didn't say anything because there were too many Halloweens when I wanted to be something, like Cinderella or a mermaid, but I didn't think I could, because I never saw one that was black. Stuff like that happens, and no matter how good friends we are, you're never going to know what it's like to be black."

"No, but we know what you're like," Kathy said seriously. "You're great."

Jill smiled at her.

"I gotta tell you guys something," Lia said slowly. "I really wanted to let you know what was going on with me, and being embarrassed wasn't the only reason I didn't. I was afraid you wouldn't like me anymore," Lia said in a small voice. "I'm not all that popular in Maple Park. Not like I was at camp. I worried that maybe you'd come here and see why and figure everyone was right."

As the girls listened intently, she told them all about Eden and how she had gathered the seventh-grade girls into her own private army, and how much she depended on Scott when everyone else seemed to disappear. "When this stupid making-out rumor started, things got so bad, it was like I was beyond un-popular. I still don't know who I'm going to hang out with when you're gone."

"There's Scott," Kathy reminded her.

"Yeah, but it's not the same as having girlfriends."

"And Missy," Erin said.

"Missy?"

"Missy told me tonight how much she liked you," Erin told Lia. "And when I asked her who Eden was, she said, 'Somebody I'm getting real tired of.' "

"She did?" Lia asked, brightening.

"Maybe you've got a new friend after all," Kathy said.

"Why does this friend stuff have to be so compli-cated?" Lia wanted to know. "We all like each other but it gets mixed up because we're not all the same color. Or the same sex. Or maybe I like someone you don't like."

"I don't see what the big deal is," Maddy said, reaching for another brownie.

"You don't?" Jill asked.

"No. If you like someone, be friends with them. If

you don't, don't. Who cares if they're boys, or black, or white, or whatever?"

Lia stared at Maddy. Could this possibly be as simple as Maddy was making it?

Later, after a lot more talking about everything from school to clothes to parents, the girls got so tired they couldn't stay up anymore. They had all gotten into their sleeping bags and were snuggling down in their beds, when Lia said, "Can I ask one more thing?"

"No," the girls chorused.

In a few minutes the room quieted down, but Lia was restless. She looked over at Jill, who was in the sleeping bag next to her. Jill was awake, too.

"Jill, do you think Maddy was right?" Lia whispered. "What she said about just picking people you like to be friends with, I mean."

Jill thought about it. "It sounds good, but things are more complicated than that."

Lia closed her eyes. "Maybe it isn't that easy." But as she drifted off to sleep, she mumbled, "But maybe it doesn't have to be as hard as we make it, either."

"I heard that," Kathy said. "I don't know how easy it is to be friends with other people, but it's pretty easy to be friends with you."

"Hey, quit it," Erin said, her voice muffled. "I'm going to start crying."

Everyone was awake enough to laugh.

"So we're still the Holiday Five?" Maddy asked with a yawn.

Lia closed her eyes. "See you at Christmas."